"I'm Going To Make Love To You, Antonia. Here. Now."

Antonia stood utterly still before Ross, her gaze meeting his. "Will it be love, Ross?"

"Would it frighten you if it were?"

"It would frighten me only if it weren't." Antonia's voice was a ragged undertone, avoiding the word *love* as if it were part of a make-believe world.

"Don't be afraid, Antonia. We're here, we're alive, and nothing could be more real than this. I love you. I think that I've loved you for a long time."

Ross drew her to him. He bent to kiss the curve of her shoulder and the hollow of her throat. Reveling in his touch, Antonia clung to him.

He said he loved her. The words were sweet music to her ears. But it was the look in his eyes, sweeter than any words, that was music to her heart. He spoke of time, but time had stopped for Antonia. Yesterday and tomorrow were no longer real....

Dear Reader,

Let's talk about summer—those wonderful months of June, July and August, when the weather warms up and Silhouette Desire stays hot.

June: Here is where you'll find another dynamite romance about the McLachlan brothers—this time Ross—by BJ James (look for more brothers later in the year!), a *Man of the Month* by Barbara Boswell, and another installment in the *Hawk's Way* series by Joan Johnston.

July: Don't look now but it's the *Red, White and Blue* heroes! These men are red-blooded, white-knight, blue-collar guys, and I know you'll love all of them! Look for the hero portrait on each and every one of these books.

August: It's a *Man of the Month* from Diana Palmer, a story from Dixie Browning and another delightful tale from Lass Small...and that's just a *tiny* amount of what's going on in August.

Yes, I think summer's going to be pretty terrific, and in the meantime I want to ask you all some questions. What do you think of the Desire line? Is there anything you'd particularly like to see that we don't provide? No answer is too outrageous; I *want* to hear your opinions.

So write and let me know. And yes, I really do exist! I'm not just some made-up name that goes on the bottom of these letters.

Until next month, happy reading,

Lucia Macro
Senior Editor

BJ JAMES
PRIDE AND PROMISES

SILHOUETTE *Desire*

™ Published by Silhouette Books New York

America's Publisher of Contemporary Romance

SILHOUETTE BOOKS
300 East 42nd St., New York, N.Y. 10017

PRIDE AND PROMISES

Copyright © 1993 by BJ James

ISBN: 0-373-05789-X

First Silhouette Books printing June 1993

All the characters in this book have no existence outside the imagination of the author and have no relation whatsoever to anyone bearing the same name or names. They are not even distantly inspired by any individual known or unknown to the author, and all incidents are pure invention.

® and ™:Trademarks used with authorization. Trademarks indicated with ® are registered in the United States Patent and Trademark Office, the Canada Trade Mark Office and in other countries.

Printed in the U.S.A.

Books by BJ James

Silhouette Desire

The Sound of Goodbye #332
Twice in a Lifetime #396
Shiloh's Promise #529
Winter Morning #595
Slade's Woman #672
A Step Away #692
Tears of the Rose #709
The Man with the Midnight Eyes #751
Pride and Promises #789

BJ JAMES

married her high school sweetheart straight out of college and soon found that books were delightful companions during her lonely nights as a doctor's wife. But she never dreamed she'd be more than a reader, never expected to be one of the blessed, letting her imagination soar, weaving magic of her own.

BJ has twice been honored by the Georgia Romance Writers with their prestigious Maggie Award for Best Short Contemporary Romance. She has also received the *Romantic Times* Critic's Choice Award.

Prologue

"No. Can't be! It's impossible."

"Who else could she be?"

"Another beautiful woman. Atlanta has its share."

"She was here before."

"Alone? Never!"

Whispers rippled through the garden restaurant, hushed accompaniment for the plaintive lament of a Hungarian violin. Heads turned, eyes glanced discretely past tree and shrub and dancing fall of water. Far from the whispers and the music, by the murmuring fountain, a lone diner sat, glass in hand, staring through the crystal dome of the roof. Beyond her the night sky was dark, strewn with brilliant stars of a southern winter night.

One carefully groomed and manicured hand lifted, the glass touched briefly against soft, full lips. Her head tipped, hair as black as the wing of a nighthawk flowed like a river down her back. The long line of her throat arched. A sip of wine had never been so graceful, so sensual.

The glass was set aside, her napkin touched lightly to her lips. Her steady gaze never left the sky.

Her face was the perfect oval, with brows a dark, graceful sweep over serious gray eyes. Beneath dusky skin high cheekbones flowed into hollows and shadow, a photographer's dream. Her gown was simple. A creation in silver and blue, enticing with understatement, revealing as it concealed.

A magnificent gown. A magnificent body.

Beyond the sip of wine she didn't move. Those who watched her utter stillness knew she did not hear their whispers, or see their interest. Their silent questions went unanswered, their curiosity unsated. They could only ponder the solitary, melancholy woman.

Who was she? Could she be who she seemed? And what fascinated in the night sky?

Without prelude, in a slow glissade of long legs and gleaming silk stockings, she stood, tossing a black fur over her shoulder. Her path to the door was without obstacle. As she passed each table, admiring eyes were lowered in deference. The well-bred who would not stare were left with an intriguing memory of a haunting scent of moss and wild roses. And, one could almost swear, of wood smoke.

At a tall marble-topped counter she paused. Stillness seemed to cling to her even as she took Madame Zara's hand in hers. Into the murmur of speech and the sigh of mournful music, came her low, throaty voice. "As always, old friend, a respite from the storm."

From her stool overlooking the garden, Madame Zara, benevolent sovereign, ruled her domain. Now, with the pure white coronet of her hair gleaming like a crown, she looked down at the young woman whose smile touched only her lips. The ancient Magyar's gesture encompassed both the sky shimmering over the roof and Atlanta's crowded streets below. "Respite from the storm out there." She touched a drape of silver that lay over a young aching heart. "But never here."

The smile again, beneath solemn eyes. "Never."

Madame Zara stroked the shining mane as black as her own was white. Brushing it from a shadowed temple, her fingertips found what they sought. A scar, livid, jagged, ugly. "He will come."

"No." Gray eyes glittered but there were no tears.

"Yes." Arthritic fingers lingered a moment longer at the scar, then moved away. "As surely as you wear the mark of valor, he will come." She shook her head, denying dispute. "Not today. Not tomorrow. Not here. But he will come." A compassionate smile too young for the aged face shone through myriad wrinkles. "When you are ready, he will come."

"You've been right so often." Strong young fingers gripped the blue veined hand. An unconscious gesture sent a ribbon of dark hair tumbling over the scar. "But not this time."

"Hear me!" The old voice held an uncommon note of entreaty. "Hear me and believe! Before the summer ends you will sit with him at your special table."

The beautiful woman smiled then with her eyes, remembering time stolen from busy schedules. Moments spent in the privacy that was Madame Zara's gift. A new memory intruded. The light went out of her eyes, her smile died. "We won't be here. Not in summer, not in winter. Not ever again. Tonight was a private goodbye. Tomorrow I go on with my life."

"He will come."

"No." Quietly. Adamant. "He won't come. We won't be back." Releasing the frail hand of her friend she stepped back.

With a gesture of farewell and a hint of a small sad smile, she turned away. Her back was straight, her head high as she walked to the door. Clutching the fur around her, she paused there for one last look. Her gaze roamed the room, touching, lingering, committing to memory again the old memories it held.

Her breasts rose in a deep breath, keeping the familiar fragrances. It was the flowers she would remember. The tiny ones nestled beneath the shrubs. Violets, trillium, anemone, pansies.

Lily of the valley.

His favorite.

His.

The room blurred. For a moment she saw the dance of a dying fire. And, listening for his laughter, waited for his arms to guard her from the cold. She drew a second breath, long and ragged. Her perfect face was bleak, as pale as alabaster. Tears that would never fall clung to her lashes.

There was no fire, no laughter, and she would never be warm again.

Suddenly aware of the whispers, the hidden looks, she squared her shoulders. Playing to an audience for the first time in the evening, her head lifted a regal inch. Her goodbyes were done, there was no reason to tarry.

With a shattering heart and a flourish of mink, she stepped through the door into the rest of her empty life.

One

He stood on the fringe, a quiet, distant figure with his back against a rough-hewn wall. There was music he didn't hear and dancers whose smiles he didn't see.

Ross McLachlan was alone in a crowded room, lost in memories of another time.

Twenty-two years had passed since the day he'd stood in this building, seeing it for the first time, hearing the brother he'd never known refuse to give up a wind scoured farm to the vagabond father they shared.

Twenty-two years since a day of revelation and surprise.

Ross smiled. If Dare was a surprise to him, then for Dare the sudden appearance of his father and a gangly, dirty street kid with two baby boys in tow must have been devastating. Three brothers! Surprise, shock, or more, it hadn't mattered, not to Dare. With integrity taught to him by Flora McLachlan, the proud Scots grandmother who'd raised him, he'd faced down their prodigal father.

Dare had kept the land his beloved Gran had bequeathed him. And, in the end, his newfound brothers as well.

Ross understood then the real meaning of honor. And, standing within the walls of a dusty old barn, a child made

old by the burden of responsibility and a temporal existence, discovered a heritage.

He was eleven that day, Dare twenty, the twins, Robert
Bruce and Jamie, less than a year. The barn, a relic of the
dream of Lachlan, first of the clan to settle in Carolina, had
stood for nearly two hundred years. While generations of
McLachlans lived and died in the shadow of its walls, it had
been shelter to the animals, storage for crops wrested from
rocky hillsides, and once, sanctuary for the family as howl-
ing red men danced in the light of burning homesteads.

Time had brought peace but not prosperity. One Mc-
Lachlan after another had deserted the land. The highland
farm of an adventurer's dream withered and died in the dust
of thin, rocky soil. The barn endured, a silent sentinel of
pride that, like it, would not die. Years beneath the blazing
sun of summer and brutal winds of winter lent burnished
dignity to stone and wood while it waited. Until again in its
shadows, driven by the stubborn determination of another
daring McLachlan, the farm lived. And four motherless
brothers became a family.

For a time, years after the day Ross had considered the
beginning of his real life, with Dare's innovations and em-
bracing of modern methods, modern buildings and modern machinery, the barn had been abandoned. Now, by the
hand and vision of this twentieth-century adventurer, it had
risen to its greatest majesty. With a dream as bold as Lachlan, Dare had stripped away every cobweb, every molder-
ing wisp of hay, laying brick tiles for the floor and filling
doorways with massive expanses of glass. Skylights set in a
towering roof captured the perfect light. In a great fireplace a fire blazed, reminding that spring, with all her ca-
price, was but one day old.

Through love an ancient structure was transformed, and
what Dare began Jacinda, his wife, his love, continued. It
was she who worked here, her paintings that hung on the
rough walls. With color and line, with symmetry and perception, she added a new dignity and grace. Her own.

Nestled in emerald fields of evergreen, a rubble of stone
became its own work of art. Blending antiquity with con-

temporary in a testament of devotion, this was its finest hour.

Today there were no cattle, no Indians. The only shadows falling over the lawn were cast by the sun of spring's new day. The sound within its walls was of revelry and laughter, as McLachlans and friends of McLachlans gathered to celebrate with a christening of the birth of a new generation—Dare and Jacinda's son and daughter.

This was as it should be, Ross felt, a celebration of the future within walls that held memories of the past. One he must attend in mind as well as body.

Smiling a charming smile, a rogue's smile, and shaking free of his reverie he turned his attention to the sprawling room and a crowd so astonishingly eclectic it defied reason that they could be friends. In the sweep of a glance he saw student, teacher, grizzled spy master and his recycled spy, potter, sculptor, engineer, pianist, actor, model, entrepreneur, canny forester, lovely painter.

And an actress.

His gaze stopped, lingered. As if sensing his scrutiny, her head lifted, her eyes finding his. Held by her magnificent gray gaze, Ross leaned lazily against the stone, one hand in the pocket of his tailored trousers, the other lifting a half filled flute of champagne.

A toast made in mockery of all he scorned.

She was still, quiet, her rarely inanimate face blank as she absorbed the impact of his satirical homage. Her level gaze never flickered, seeming to look straight through him, denying his existence. Then, as if drawing herself from her thoughts, she inclined her head. A slight move, barely discernible, that accepted and dismissed his barb.

As one would inspect a boring misfit, her stare moved slowly down the length of him and with cool deliberation, back again to the perfectly knotted tie at his throat and the classic cashmere jacket lying over heavy shoulders. Ross braced for a derisive laugh, the haughty condescension. Instead she went very still. Stiller than before. Her hands were folded stiffly in her lap and not even a breath stirred the clinging, smoky amethyst of her gown.

Only a frown drew tiny lines over her forehead as her eyes bored into his as if seeing him for the first time. Almost reluctantly her thoughtful attention turned to his mouth. Her breasts rose in a sharp breath drawn, held. An expression he couldn't fathom flickered over her perfect features, then with a sigh and a shake of her head it was gone.

The baffling moment was done. Antonia turned away, her reprisal left unfinished.

Or was it? Ross wondered. Was her strange reaction a new tactic in a long-running skirmish? Insult deferred, to intrigue, to prove that even in his aversion he was not immune to the fascination of a beautiful woman?

"Good try, sweetheart," Ross murmured and then he laughed. Framed by the glare of towering windows, his face alight with wry amusement, he continued his languid study of the most glittering of this glittering gala.

Four years ago Jacinda Talbot had come to the valley to make a new life for herself and Tyler, the child she'd inherited at the death of one of her many stepsisters. Once in each of those years Antonia swept into Madison to visit, sparing a steadfast friend an hour or two on her way from one exotic location to another. Antonia, with designer dresses clinging to a perfect body, tossing her gleaming mane of ebony about exquisite shoulders.

A temptress whose maddening scent trailed ever behind her in subtle reminder. Lest one dared forget, that Antonia Russell, star of stage and screen, had passed by.

Today, rising to the occasion, she'd stayed for more than an hour, more than two, and this small part of Madison had become her stage. Playing the role of godmother to the hilt she'd drawn her audience in, holding them with her level gaze, her interest. She enchanted, captivated, beguiled, until the imaginary became real. Until she became real and every male, innocent and jaded alike, worshiped at her shrine.

Only Ross was immune. Only his attentions were unwelcome.

From their first meeting on Dare and Jacinda's wedding day the battle lines had been drawn. Judgments made never wavered—she was self-centered, a pampered narcissist; he, a boring provincial, for all his education and thriving pediatric practice, a backwoods hick.

With sarcasm as weapon of choice, a subtle war was declared. Four years and four short, caustic encounters later, Antonia was still glamorous tinsel and he a redneck buffoon. Her claws were steel beneath the velvet. His contempt biting, a rapier's point.

Nothing changed. Ross was sure it never would.

Except, he thought, making a rare concession, this trip she seemed less flamboyant, quieter, softer. Something sensed more than seen. In the midst of the christening she'd calmed a frightened baby with a soothing word, an awkward but gentle caress. And he'd found himself almost liking her.

Almost, he amended, shying away from the incredible admission. "An act," he muttered putting his empty glass aside. His scowling gaze returned to Antonia. "Only an act, what she does best."

"Taken up talking to yourself, have you?" a familiar voice asked as a hand slid through the bend of his arm. "If you must, talk, but don't frown, it causes wrinkles." Then in the same breath she said, innocently, "But she is beautiful, isn't she?"

"Who?"

"Ross!" The rebuke was gentle, the laughter indulgent.

"No," he began from habit then stopped. It was as ridiculous to lie as to pretend ignorance. Antonia was beautiful. So beautiful it took his breath away. "Yes." The terse admission was uttered through grimly clenched teeth. "She's beautiful."

"Ah, progress! Once you wouldn't have admitted even that little bit."

Shrugging aside the comment, he looked down at the small woman at his side, his bearing altering dramatically. There was affection, not mockery, in his voice as he amended his concession. "Beautiful, yes, but not in your class."

Jacinda McLachlan laughed again. "There are times I suspect an Irishman hidden in your family tree. One who kissed the blarney stone."

"Could be. We've been known to stretch a point or two on occasions."

Jacinda chuckled. "On occasions like now."

Ross ignored her droll interpretation. "If you don't believe you're the most beautiful woman in this room, ask Dare."

"Dare's prejudiced. He's supposed to be. What's your excuse?"

"No excuse, just a man who knows his own mind."

"Do you?" Jacinda leveled a suddenly solemn look at him. "Do you really?"

His smile faded. "What does that mean?"

"It means..." Jacinda paused, then shook her head. "Never mind. This isn't the time."

"What time, Jacinda?" The low voice was like the woman who spoke, sultry, provocative, memorable.

"Is this a private conversation, or can anyone join in?"

Ross's hooded gaze lifted to the intruder. His cold look moved from her, to the deserted corner where she'd held court, then back again. A significant beat later he drawled, "Lose your audience, sweetheart?"

Antonia Russell laughed softly, a husky, lazy note. "Jealous, Doc?"

"Hardly. One doesn't fall victim to the fever when immune to the disease."

Antonia laughed again, the same husky note accompanied by the gentle arching of one brow. "I've been called a lot of things by a lot of men, but never a fever."

"I'll bet you have." Ross's face was a study in granite. His attention was so riveted on Antonia he didn't feel Jacinda's hand slide from his arm.

"But you're immune." Antonia lifted her head, her dark hair tumbling around her shoulders.

"Forever." Blue eyes dueled with gray. Neither wavered.

"Are you, Doc?" Antonia took a step closer, running a polished nail up his patterned tie to the hint of a cleft in his chin. "I wonder, are you really? Do you ever truly forget that I'm a woman?" Then with a long drawn breath she murmured, "Can you?"

"Oh, I never forget, I'll give you that. But what man could? Even if you didn't work so hard to make sure of it." Ross caught her hand in his, holding it in a hard grip. "Let's just say you're not my type, sugar, and leave it at that."

Undaunted by the jeer and ignoring the crush of her fingers, with her free hand Antonia stroked the shaggy hair from his forehead. Her nails tracing a lazy line down his nape and back again to his hair, she asked huskily, "What is your type? What turns the good Dr. McLachlan on?"

In a parody of her own words Ross sidestepped the question. "Jealous, sweetheart?"

With exaggerated care Antonia continued to smooth his hair above the collar of his shirt, her chuckle ending with a long, regretful sigh. "Sorry, Doc, just curious."

Jacinda looked from one to the other with a pleased look on her face. As discreetly as she could she took a step back, leaving the arena to Ross.

Ross didn't notice. In a sunlit room, filled with music and firelight, Antonia commanded his fierce regard. Flinging his head back from her teasing caress, his grip tightened over her captured hand. In their island of quiet no lash fluttered over burning eyes. Neither blue stare nor gray yielded.

Ross was first to speak. "You're so sure you have me pegged, you tell me. What is my type, sweetheart? What turns me on?"

A look flashed in Antonia's eyes, a look of ungoverned confusion. A faltering so minute, recovered so quickly, Ross wondered if he'd only imagined the shattering of the perfect illusion. With a flutter of downcast lashes a shutter came down and she was as always, assured, controlled, aloof. Yet as he cursed, bitterly, his faithless body's response to her teasing, he couldn't quite dispel the haunting feeling that he'd caught a rare glimpse of a vulnerable woman beneath the cold luster of glamour.

In that unguarded moment had he seen a woman he hadn't believed existed? A real woman who could comfort a crying child and turn from a mocking toast with something akin to regret.

"Antonia," he began and had no idea what he meant to say, no idea why he wanted to apologize. No idea why he should.

His jeering question forgotten, he held her hand in his against the cashmere jacket. The music became a sonata, hushed and beautiful. Jamie the youngest McLachlan sat at the piano, playing as only he could. From the fireplace the scent of wood smoke rose to mingle with a whisper of moss and wild roses. Antonia's scent.

Antonia, with the sun falling through skylights, flooding over her, scattering black diamonds in her hair.

Dear God she was beautiful. He hadn't realized how beautiful until now. He hadn't felt the dark mystical appeal that beckoned and beguiled, until now. Ross's gut clenched. Confusing thoughts became a smoldering need. One neither mind nor body could deny.

He touched her hair, wanting to gather diamonds in his palm. His voice was low, hoarse. "Antonia."

"Yes." Her heavy lashes drifted to her cheeks shielding her eyes once more. "Antonia." Her solemn gaze lifted to his. A siren looked through flashing silver eyes, the seductress whose wiles proved her power. "Antonia turns you on."

"No." The lie was strained as her irony turned cold the fire in him.

"Lies won't change it, Ross." Her gentle tone mocked him. "I'm everything you condemn." Her fingertips found the pulse at his temple. "Here." Her palm cupped his cheek for a second then glided to his chest, her fingers sliding beneath their joined hands to cashmere that lay over his heart.

"Ah, but here?" Her laugh was a velvet purr, conveying more than words, more than a contemptuous toast. "Nothing you can say, nothing you can do, can dismiss me so easily *here*."

"Can't I?" Ross's face was grim, but there was grudging admiration in his voice. She was good, he'd give her that. The little flashes, the fathomless looks were all part of her game. He hadn't seen the gentle woman beneath the performer's facade. That creature existed only as another facet of her skill and was no more credible than this little seduction. Clasping both her hands in his he held them tightly to his chest. Even his most mischievous little patients had never looked so guileless.

All right, she'd drawn him in, hoisting him on his own petard. The first skirmish was hers. Perhaps he deserved what she'd done, he conceded, but the war was far from over. If Antonia's look was innocent, his sudden grin was more than wicked.

A wariness flickered over her face, turning her smile to a narrow-eyed frown. Through lowered lashes she watched him closely, waiting.

Ross shook his head, making vague sounds of regret. "I'm sorry, sweetheart."

The gentle words, the tender tone, not the response she expected, caught her unprepared. Her frown deepened. "You're sorry?"

His earnest gaze held hers. "I didn't know."

"You didn't know?" The wariness was back, this time tempered by curiosity.

"I didn't realize how sadly lacking your education has been."

"My education has served me nicely, thank you."

"I guess you just don't know then."

"But I'm sure you're going to tell me," Antonia drawled.

"It's your geography."

"What about my geography?"

A regretful sigh, a frown. "Atrocious."

"Atrocious, huh?" She drew away from him, waiting for the punch line. One hand rested on her hip. The other tapped an exaggerated tattoo against her wrist. "Suppose you tell me what a backwoods hick knows about geography that I don't."

"I thought you'd never ask."

"Now I have. So—" she gestured impatiently "—why don't you tell me?"

"Glad to, but maybe I'd better clarify that anatomy is a better word than geography."

Antonia nodded curtly, suspecting the tables had been turned. She'd been as skillfully drawn in by a ruse as Ross.

But Ross wasn't ready to make his point. Instead he took another slow survey of Antonia's geography, seeing her through the eyes of the millions of men who adored her.

Beneath hair that was blacker than sin and just as enticing, her features were more classic than pretty. Black brows swept like a raven's wing over eyes he'd only recently discovered could go from sultry, smoldering gray to sparkling, teasing silver in the throb of a pulse. The slash of high cheekbones and the delicate hollows beneath drew attention to a generous mouth. Framed by a strong, rounded chin and the heavy tumble of careless curls, sensual lips invited a man's kiss.

She was tall. Not enough to tower over her leading men, but enough to allow long, lean spaces between curves that set a man's mouth hungering to explore. Then there were her legs. Long glorious legs that not even the filmy fabric that made him think of the haze that hovered over mountains on a shadowy day could hide. Only a monk wouldn't wonder what it would be like to have them wrapped around him, holding him.

Hell, even he wondered.

"You're right, sweetheart," he said at last. His inspection done, his lazy look tangled with hers, letting her read his thoughts. "You turn a man on. Can't deny that." Bending from the waist he leaned closer, his lips almost touching hers. "But it's another part of his anatomy you excite, not his heart."

He laughed and chucked her under her chin as he would one of his tiny patients. "That's your geography lesson for this year. See you next year, on your next visit.

"Jacinda." Ross turned, gathering the smaller woman's hands in his, bringing them to his lips to kiss her fingertips. "Thank you for the privilege of being godfather to my niece and nephew. I question the wisdom of your choice of godmother, but who am I to judge?"

"Are you leaving already?" Jacinda's amusement faded abruptly.

"Only long enough to make some checks on the plane. I leave for New York tomorrow."

"Your conference, I'd forgotten." Jacinda held his hands, looking into the face that was so much like Dare's, so much like the twins'. A strong face, weathered and tanned, with a mouth meant to smile. And ice blue eyes that hid the bruises of a lost child. The hurt he never spoke of.

Of Dare's brothers she worried most about Ross. Her heart ached more for him. Blinking back an unexpected prickle of tears she asked sternly, "You'll be back for dinner?"

"If you wish."

"I wish."

"Then count on it." He kissed her cheek. "I'll be back before you know it."

Without a glance toward Antonia he left them, the best of friends standing together, watching as he treaded through the crowd to the door.

Two

_____

"**H**e's insufferable."

A student moonlighting as waiter stopped by with a tray of canapés. Antonia took one, and then as he waited, another. Jacinda smothered a laugh. Antonia never ate canapés.

Biting into a round of bread topped with a tiny shrimp, Antonia chewed absently. Grumbling, she devoured both pretty little morsels.

"He thought he would annoy me, but it didn't quite work."

"Uh-huh." Jacinda's noncommittal response was accompanied by a half-hidden smile.

"Backwoods dolt!"

"Backwoodsman," Jacinda corrected. "But not a dolt."

"There's a difference?"

"Absolutely."

"Do tell me more," Antonia drawled in wry distaste.

"It would serve you right if I did. And maybe someday I will. Or better yet, maybe you'll discover the difference for yourself."

"Not if I can run fast enough. A backwoodsman!"

"There are worse things to be," Jacinda was adamant. "And other than a McLachlan and a pediatrician, Ross had never wanted to be anything else."

"He's arrogant."

"Yes."

"Opinionated."

"I know."

"Obstinate."

"Runs in the family."

"Arrogant."

"A part of the McLachlan heritage."

"A chauvinist."

"Sometimes." Jacinda nodded.

"With an ego as big as...as..." A satisfying analogy escaped Antonia.

"Yours?"

"Yes. No!" A quick unthinking response. Then only mildly outraged, "This from my friend?"

"Sorry." Jacinda shrugged.

After a long silence, Antonia chuckled. "You've always had a knack for calling a spade a spade."

"Sorry," Jacinda said again.

"Don't be. I need someone to do it."

"Someone other than Ross."

"Ross," Antonia said emphatically, "is insufferable."

"You're repeating yourself."

"Obstinate?"

"You said that."

"Arrogant?"

Jacinda held up two fingers. "Twice."

"Conceited?"

"That's a new one." Jacinda waited for the next outburst, but there was none. "Finished?"

"Yeah." A smile defeated Antonia's attempt to maintain a grim face. "I guess I am."

Jacinda linked her arm through Antonia's. Jamie's sonata drifted into blues. A baby cried and was soothed by his father's touch.

Antonia turned impulsively to Jacinda. "I'll be a good godmother, Jacinda. The best, I promise."

"I know. That's why we asked you, and why we delayed the christening until you were free."

"I don't know very much about babies, but I can learn. I know I called them ugly little squiggly things, but it was just...ah..."

"An uninformed generality?" Jacinda offered.

"Exactly! Babies are wonderful."

"So long as they belong to someone else."

"Well, yes." Antonia looked worriedly down at her friend. "But I'll be good."

"You don't have to convince me, Antonia. I chose you, remember?" Struggling to keep a straight face Jacinda patted her glamorous friend's bejeweled hand. "I asked you to be godmother, not mother. It's not quite the same."

"Like the difference between backwoodsman and dolt?"

Jacinda laughed. "Not quite."

"Well whatever, I'll be good. *No!*" Antonia lapsed into an old, almost forgotten habit of speaking in italics, revealing all over again how strongly Ross's barbs had hit home. "I'll be great. More than great. I'll be *terrific!* Ross McLachlan doesn't know everything!"

"No," Jacinda agreed mildly, "but he is handsome, isn't he?"

From beneath the fringe of black lashes and lifted brows Antonia's gray gaze narrowed. Then she grinned. Jacinda had slipped that sly little jewel in nicely. "Yes," she admitted grudgingly, "he is. For a backwoods hick." Then, after a long pause she said, "Backwoodsman. Dammit!"

Jacinda was the first to laugh. Then both were giggling, as they had as schoolgirls.

"Now that we agree on that—" Jacinda wiped the laughter from her face "—maybe we should join the others. They must be wondering what our little tête-à-tête was all about."

"What they're wondering is who came away with the most bruises this time, Ross or me," Antonia commented dryly as she was steered toward the group where Paul Talbot was speaking expansively of his days on the stage and screen.

"Who did?" Jacinda wondered aloud.

"Beats me."

"But you'll live to fight another day."

Antonia wrapped an arm around Jacinda's shoulders. "I hope so. What would I do for entertainment in this godforsaken paradise if I couldn't bedevil your handsome husband's brother?"

"I think I know."

Antonia stopped dead still, her arm falling from Jacinda. "What the hell does that mean?"

"What does what mean?" The garbled line was delivered with the studied innocence of a straight man.

Antonia shot her a suddenly suspicious look. "Good grief, Jacinda! You aren't matchmaking!" There was a doubtful pause, then she said, "Are you?"

"Who? Me?" Jacinda's smile was angelic. "Never."

"Jacinda, darling! Antonia! Come join us." Paul Talbot interrupted, waving them into the group clustered near the fire. He watched, beaming with fatherly pride as Dare kissed Jacinda tenderly, relinquished the baby he held, then drew both into his arms.

"Tell me, Antonia," Paul demanded. "What do you think of my grandchildren?" Bending over the chair at his side, with a perfectly manicured finger he stroked the cheek of the baby boy who slept in Tyler's lap. "Amy's as pretty as her mother and young Paul's a chip off the old block, wouldn't you say?"

"Exactly." Antonia agreed but offered a silent prayer that all young Paul would have in common with his grandfather was his name and his looks. Paul Talbot was undeniably a handsome man. He hadn't been a bad actor, either, just a man born too soon. In another era he would've been in his element. Swashbuckler extraordinaire among swashbucklers. As it was, he'd never been very successful, in his profession or his six marriages. His only success was his daughter, Jacinda.

And for Jacinda Antonia could forgive Paul Talbot anything. "All of Jacinda's children are splendid." With a touch that included six-year-old Tyler, bringing a gap-toothed smile to his face, and a look at Jacinda she added, "As splendid as their mother."

"Well said, sweetheart." A warmed breath fanned her ear and a tanned hand offered a flute of champagne. "Shall we drink to it?"

As she faced him, Antonia didn't think to question when Ross had returned, nor why he had two glasses at just the appropriate time. All she saw was that for the first time in four years, there was no mockery in his smile.

While fresh glasses were found and Jamie, the youngest of the original McLachlan twins, poured champagne, Ross waited at her side. With their glasses filled, one by one each guest turned to Ross.

They were all present, all the friends who played important roles in Dare and Jacinda's lives.

The Canfields. Raven, Dare's friend since childhood, and David who came to the valley a man bitter from the horrors of a life of secrecy and danger and found love as well as peace.

The Slades. Hunter, the once reclusive half-breed sculptor, and his lovely Beth, who walked with him into the world.

The McCallums. Patrick, a man as fair and loyal as he was brutal, whose business empire was far-flung and his friendships deep. A man whose eyes rarely strayed from Jordana, the gentle woman who tamed him, and whose stunning blind eyes would never see him.

Patrick's second in command, a dark, dangerous man with a startling sense of humor, who guarded his friendships with his life.

Simon McKinsey, a granite tower of a man. A man of unusual honor, who dealt in the secret protection of his country. Who in this visit exhibited a puzzling interest in Jamie.

The families. Paul Talbot, Robert Bruce and Jamie. And lastly, Tyler, whose very existence brought Jacinda to Madison and to Dare.

There were others, students, teachers, neighbors, but these were the special friends. Friends who had come from all over the world to share this special day with the McLachlans. Dare's friends, with one exception, who welcomed Jacinda into their circle and became hers as well.

The exception, Antonia. The one friend Jacinda had brought with her into her new life. The exotic bird of paradise with a streak of loyalty buried deeply in her calculating heart.

Because of that loyalty, because she meant so much to Jacinda, Ross could forget the animosity that seethed between them. He'd gotten only as far as his car when he turned back, his decision made. For this one special day he would offer Antonia the hand of peace.

All eyes were on him now, waiting expectantly. Antonia's reserved gaze among them. Lifting his glass Ross spoke from his heart. "To Dare, brother and friend, who brought an ancient dream to reality. To Jacinda, who brought him the love he deserves.

"And to Tyler—" he smiled down at the boy "—who brought them together. Without whom this celebration wouldn't be. McLachlans and friends, I give you the new generation. Tyler, Amy and Paul."

"The new generation," Patrick echoed and was the first to drink from his glass.

"And to peace," Ross murmured to Antonia, leaning close, letting the clean, fresh scent of her shining hair surround him. "Just for today."

Startled by his closeness, his words, Antonia's hand halted abruptly halfway to her lips, the bubbling wine threatening to spill over her wrist. Searching for some ulterior motive she looked up at him, her serious gaze unwavering. For a long while she was silent, wary.

"A truce between us, a gift for Dare and Jacinda on their special day," Ross persuaded.

Antonia was distrustful.

"Just until after dinner. Then we go our separate ways. The next time we meet it can be with sabers drawn."

"But for now, pleasantries instead of insults?"

"Yes."

"Can you do it? Can I?"

"We're intelligent adults, Antonia, we can do anything wo set our minds to."

"No tricks?" Antonia remembered, if Ross didn't, that just a while ago he had, in circuitous fashion, questioned her intelligence.

"No tricks."

"Promise."

"On the heads of our son and daughter."

"Godson and goddaughter," Antonia corrected distractedly.

"Of course." Ross accepted the correction with a gallant bow.

"All right, then." She drew a much needed breath as the walls of mistrust came down. "A truce, until dinner is done. As a gift for Dare and Jacinda."

"To peace." Ross smiled then, and touched his glass to hers. "And to my beautiful dinner companion."

Antonia recoiled, on guard at the unaccustomed compliment.

Startled that her distrust was so easily resurrected, Ross extended his hand offering the only assurance he could. "A promise with my word and my hand on it, Antonia. My proof of peace, and an admission that even to me you're beautiful."

Her look was guileless, and evident in it, her need to believe.

Ross smiled, his hand open and waiting for hers. "It's all I have to give, sweetheart."

Antonia hesitated only a moment longer before taking his hand, holding it in hers. "It's enough. And thank you for the compliment. Coming from you it means more than..." Stopping she looked down at their joined hands.

"More than what, Antonia?"

When she looked up she was smiling, her pensive mood gone. "More than your insults, of course."

"Of course." Then both were laughing, not one at the other, but together.

"Ross." Raven Canfield touched his arm to gain his attention. "You have a call. Carolyn Elliot. Her youngest has a temperature again."

"Thanks, Raven. I'll be right along." Drawing his hand from Antonia's he stepped away. "Charlie's one of my kids who's prone to have tonsillitis. I'll have to see him, but I'll be back for dinner. Can't let this truce go to waste."

"I'll be waiting." Antonia was surprised that she really meant it. As Raven walked away with Ross, she assured herself she was only looking forward to discovering what this mercurial man called a truce. "That," she said to no one in particular, "should be very interesting."

When would it end? Antonia wondered. The evening that had shown such promise had turned sour.

Her fault, not Ross's, she admitted. Drawing a slow, long breath and then another, she was grateful the veranda was deserted. No prying and pitying eyes to see her weakness.

With one hand gripping a railing and the other fisted, pressing against her breasts, she struggled with the invisible weight lying like a boulder in her chest. Fighting against the urge to breathe and breathe and breathe, she couldn't think. Panic gnawed at her resilience. Fear stabbed the back of her throat. Her body clamored for oxygen it didn't need.

Shivering, she clenched her teeth and jutted her jaw. She was a fighter. Everything she'd ever had, or accomplished, she'd fought for. But how did she fight something she couldn't see, something she didn't understand? That struck, as it had tonight, without warning.

How did she fight her own body and mind? The phantom within herself.

That the phantom had a name didn't ease her fear, nor the frustration of her own infirmity. One she couldn't afford or admit, not when she was poised on the brink of true success.

Who would believe there was nothing physically wrong? Nothing that would affect her performance? The honoring of obligations?

How did she explain profound fatigue, a vague but malicious malady that had her gasping for the breaths she didn't need? Hyperventilation, overbreathing, was a truly frightening thing.

Who would understand and forgive the diagnosis made by a phalanx of learned physicians? A protracted process of elimination, confirmed by battery after battery of secret tests. Each more exotic and less conclusive than the last.

If she'd had the breath, Antonia would have laughed. A laugh that would have been bitter.

By process of elimination, it had been decreed that she was profoundly fatigued. That was the specter threatening all she'd worked to achieve. The shadow over the success that was at last within her grasp. How did one fight a shadow? What magic potion would cure the symptoms manifested by a healthy body and sound mind demanding the rest she couldn't give it?

There had been those with solutions. Wily predators whose watching eyes saw what others couldn't. The unscrupulous who thought to seduce in a moment of weakness or pain. Who offered promises of heaven and dreams realized, great power and easy confidence. The world, encased in tiny, glistening vials of white powder.

Cocaine.

Antonia hated drugs, hated the destruction, yet she shuddered now remembering one shocking moment of temptation. But only temptation.

The terror of that moment, so alien to all she believed, accomplished what weeks and months of worry and fear had not. Vowing she would never be so weak nor so desperate, she turned at last to medicine for answers.

Answer. Singular, for no matter how it was expressed, by what name it was called, it was always the same.

Exhaustion. Stress. Strain. Duress. Beat. Weary. So many names for the same nightmare. Some more colorful than others.

Battle fatigue, the bluntest, a grizzled war veteran had declared. Asking too much of the mind and body, for too long. All battles were not fought on the battlefield, he reminded. All were not life and death. All were not bloody.

A change of pace, men in wrinkled lab coats with their own fatigue etched in their faces had prescribed.

Rest, she was told time and again, was the only cure.

"I can't," she muttered aloud to the night. "Not now. Not when I'm so close."

"Talking to yourself, Antonia?"

She whirled, gasping as much for breath as in surprise. "Ross. I didn't hear you coming." Then struggling for a semblance of calm she asked, "What are you doing here? You're missing Jacinda's famous Brandy Alexander."

"There'll be others." His eyes skimmed over her. Eyes that in the moonlight held an edge of concern. "You left the table so abruptly, I thought something might be wrong."

"So you followed to see if you could help?" she asked, giving herself time to regain her equilibrium. "How gallant."

Her sarcasm didn't escape him, nor did her pallor and the trembling fist that still pressed against her breasts. "I thought you might be ill." He inclined his head. "And yes, I wondered if I could help."

"You? Help me?" She threw back her head and her breathless laugh was husky, seductive. She dared not let him see her weakness. Ross, most of all, must never know what the profession he held in contempt had done to her. In the only way she knew, she tried to divert him. Lifting her fist from her breast, she cupped her palm over his cheek. "Doc." She leaned closer, letting her scent envelop him. "Dinner's over, and our little truce."

She leaned closer still, playing the tease she knew he abhorred. Letting him think the long struggling breaths were meant to be sultry, she drew her fingers over his cheek, stopping provocatively at the corner of his mouth. Her gaze held his as he caught an involuntary gasp.

"I simply needed some air." Not completely a lie. "There's nothing you can do for me, Doc." Her laugh rang through the night like a flawed silver bell. "There's nothing I would ever want from you."

The clap of flesh against flesh resounded like a shot as his fingers closed over her wrist. "No?" He muttered dragging her hand away from his face and she to him in one move. "Nothing, Antonia?" He pulled her closer until his thighs brushed hers and her breasts teased the folds of his jacket. "Not even this?"

The last thing Antonia saw was the glitter of anger in his eyes.

His head dipped, his breath scorched her cheek and his mouth took hers. His kiss was hot and burning. A brand. Shock held her immobile. When she thought to move away, his hand was in her hair, twisting, gripping, keeping her. When she opened her mouth to draw a breath his tongue found hers, demanding and sweet, and she forgot her role.

Her hands closed around his lapels, not to push away but to hold on. Her knees were weak, her head was spinning and the soft, yielding sigh she heard was her own.

Ross heard it, too. His kiss grew gentle, his hands stroked her hair, tangled and stroked again. One slid the length of her body to curve at her hip, holding her closer. And closer still. She was silk and wild roses, shadow and sunlight, challenge and promise.

Lifting his mouth from hers he brushed a trail of kisses down her throat. With his face buried in her hair he breathed the scent of her. "Antonia," he murmured. "I—"

The strident ring of a telephone ripped the fabric of the night. Too loud. Too insistent.

Through the open doorway Dare's voice rose over the din of music and laughter. "Has anyone seen Ross? Carolyn Elliot's child is worse."

Even as quick as Ross's reflexes were, before he could re-act, Antonia was moving away. The curve of her lips was more wistful than a smile. "Duty calls, Doc."

Ross knew he had to go. Charlie needed him. Still he didn't turn or look away. Standing within the circle of her scent, within the magic of her aura, he wondered what the hell had happened. What undercurrents had his kisses stirred? What madness had driven him to forget himself? To forget what she was. What she could never be.

She touched his arm. "The telephone. Mrs. Elliot."

He shook himself from his brooding. "I'm sorry I intruded, Antonia. It won't happen again." His look was dark and forbidding as he turned away without a word.

He was nearly at the threshold of the open door when she called out. "Doc." She waited until she felt his cold blue gaze on her. "You weren't intruding. Rather than snapping at you, I should thank you for your concern. But I'm all right, truly. Just tired to put it simply, or so a battalion of physicians tell me."

Ross nodded, confirming his own speculation. "I thought it might be something of that nature."

"Stressful work, this playacting business." Her weak attempt at nonchalance fell flat. She was suddenly nervous, apologizing to Ross was a rare and difficult thing. As rare as the kiss that still warmed her lips and the quiet, lonely need it had awakened. She had to hold herself rigid to keep from shaking. "I'm sorry I goaded you."

Ross shrugged. "Except for a little while tonight, it's all we've ever done."

"Our truce."

He nodded again, waiting for Antonia to finish.

"Until now it didn't go so badly. Maybe—" she licked dry lips "—maybe next visit we could try it again." With a qualifying gesture, she added quickly, "For Jacinda's sake."

She was beautiful there in the moonlight. Even in its dark light Ross could see the flush of her cheeks against the pallor of her face. With a shock he realized he wanted to touch her again, to forget that she was everything he scorned.

Sudden anger flared white-hot and unforgiving within him. At Antonia for playing at making him want her. At himself for wanting.

It was on the tip of his tongue to tell her to get the hell away and stay away. Instead he heard a voice that was his saying, "We could try."

"For Jacinda."

"Yes," he said after a time. "For Jacinda."

"Doc."

Ross halted in midturn. "Yes?"

"How old is Charlie?"

"He's six."

"The same as Tyler."

"Three months younger."

Antonia was surprised. "You know how old all your patients are?"

"Most."

"You must be pretty good at what you do."

"I try to be, Antonia."

He would be better than good with the children. She'd seen that in how he dealt with Tyler and with Jacinda's babies. Ross was opinionated, obstinate and arrogant. But she could see that he would be wonderful with his patients, the children he fondly called his.

"About little Charlie."

"What about him, Antonia?"

"I hope he's better soon."

Ross was startled that she cared. "Thanks. So do I."

"I've kept you. You should go."

"I know." He inclined his head. In the moonlight his hair was darker and his shoulders broader. "Good night, Antonia."

Antonia watched him walk to the light. A man who could comfort a child and ease a mother's fears. A man with the strength to put aside deep-seated differences to offer comfort to an old enemy. When he stepped from sight, she touched her lips thoughtfully and turned to face the phantoms of her darkness alone.

Three

——

Jacinda sat at her dressing table drawing a brush through her hair. At the soft sound of a door closing her hand grew still, her gaze lifted finding Dare's.

"Hi," she said softly, her eyes sweeping over his mirrored image. She never tired of seeing him as he was. Naked, only a towel tucked low over his hips. His sun-darkened skin, damp from his shower, glittering with beads of moisture.

"Hi yourself, Mrs. McLachlan." He moved across the floor, his bare footsteps only a rustle over the carpet. Standing a pace behind her he took the brush, sliding it through her hair, swirling it from her neck. Bending to kiss the tender spot he'd exposed he murmured against her flesh, "The children?"

Jacinda drew a shaky breath as his mouth teased the curve of her shoulder. "All three tucked safely into bed."

"Antonia?" Dare skimmed her robe from one shoulder, letting it slide down her arm. A trail of kisses explored new territory.

"In her room, but I'm not sure she's sleeping." With her head thrown back, through half-shuttered eyes Jacinda

watched him in the mirror, reveling in the supple beauty of
sleek muscles rippling beneath taut skin and in the sorcery
of his callused fingers. Dare was a beautiful man, a man
who knew magic. "I think," she gasped, drawing in his
mingled scent of soap and evergreen as he slid the robe down
her body. The falling silk caressed her. She trembled in exquisite need as it clung like a teasing kiss to a tender nipple.
"I think," she tried again, "Antonia sleeps very little."

"Uh-huh," Dare muttered his agreement. "The excitement of battle." His laugh was a whisper over her skin.
"Helluva choice we made for godparents. Life will never be
dull, my love." He kissed his way back up one shoulder and
began to lavish the same attention on the neglected shoulder.

"They'll be good."

"Together or apart?" He asked, more interested in her
response to his explorations than his question.

As Dare nuzzled her neck and nipped at an earlobe, she
had to catch the thought that eluded her. "Both," she
managed as her world righted a bit.

"If they don't go up in flames first."

"Today was a close one."

"I know," Dare murmured into the curve of her throat.
"You were standing so close, I thought I should check for
burns."

"Is that what you're doing? Checking for burns?" Jacinda laughed.

"Among other things. How about here? And here? And
here?"

Jacinda shivered again and closed her eyes. "Antonia
seems different. She's quieter, more reserved. She's always
been so strong. Now she seems tired, vulnerable."

"Not too tired nor too vulnerable to go a second round
with Ross after dinner."

"Even that wasn't the same. When Ross came in from the
deck, there was an undercurrent."

"It's always there, my love. Just beneath the surface."

"If they'd ever stop fighting." The second shoulder was
bare. Now her gown was sliding.

"But they won't." Dare's tongue traced a slow, darting line over the ridge of her shoulder.

"Why, Dare? Why won't they?" The gown clung, too, for an eternity, tantalizing the tips of her breasts, then in a tide of silk it drifted to her waist.

"Because if they ever do..." Dare's voice was low, barely a sound. The hairbrush fell to the floor. His hands stroked down her arms to her waist, then up to her midriff, and finally, reverently, to her breasts. Holding her, caressing her, one hand glided up the gentle slope. His palm cradled her throat, his thumb lifted her face to his. "Because... if...they...ever...stop..." In repetition each measured word had its own caress, its own delight as he waited for her heavy lashes to lift. Until in her eyes he saw the passion that matched his own. "Then—" he stroked her body with unsteady hands "—they would do this."

His lips touched hers. A kiss that began like a whisper deepened to thunderous passion. With the fleeting thought that love would be like this between Ross and Antonia, Jacinda turned to Dare. Her mouth opened to his, her fingers found the towel. As it fluttered to the floor he was lifting her in his arms, striding to their bed.

"Dare!" Jacinda bolted upright, wide-awake and blissfully ignoring her nakedness.

"What is it, honey? One of the twins? Tyler?" Dare mumbled into the arm he'd thrown over his face as she snapped on the light.

"Patrick!"

That brought him fully awake. It would tend to when the woman he knew loved him with all her heart, looking wildly fetching in nothing but the afterglow of sex, muttered about a charismatic Scot. "What the hell does Patrick have to do with anything?"

"He's right."

"I'm sure he has been. Many times." Dare made a deliberate show of patience. "What is he right about this time?"

"At dinner he said stubborn people sometimes need help in admitting they love each other."

"Honey, Patrick's not exactly an expert on love."

"I know." Jacinda gestured excitedly. "That's just the point. He's an expert at being obstinate. At least he was. If Rafe hadn't tricked Jordana into going to Scotland, if he hadn't locked them in a room together, they wouldn't be married and expecting a baby today."

"He didn't lock them in a room."

"Well, he might as well have," Jacinda protested, preferring her version of the story to the truth. "If Rafe put you in a room, you'd stay, wouldn't you?"

"I suppose I would." Dare chuckled, imagining the dark and dangerous Rafe Courtenay playing cupid. As Patrick's oldest friend and trusted CEO, Rafe was the only man on earth who would've dared. "If the woman were you, and as tempting as you are now, I wouldn't have had a prayer in hell of escaping." The laughter faded, his voice roughened. "I wouldn't have tried."

"Patrick and Jordana had Rafe. Simon sent David to Raven. We had Jamie and Robbie and Ross. Someone cared." She stroked his cheek, her palm cradled his face as she leaned to him. "Because someone cared, I have you. Thank God, I have you. I want this for Ross and Antonia. This, Dare." Her trembling passion, her dreams, her love poured from her, her kiss saying more than words.

Startled, touched, Dare reached for more and found his fingertips grazing a bare, lovely bottom. Jacinda had scrambled from the bed and was scooping up the telephone. He sat up, bewildered, with the tumbled sheet draping his hips. "What on earth are you doing, Jacinda?"

"Calling Ross."

"Calling Ross," Dare repeated in an undertone. "Why, might I ask, are you calling Ross?"

"To hitch a ride to New York."

Calmly he said, "You aren't going to New York."

Jacinda dialed the number with a flourish. "Antonia is."

"Honey, you don't seriously think..."

"Ross! Hello." Her greeting was warm and vibrant as she held up a hand ending Dare's protest. "I need a favor." She paused, listening. "The babies are fine. Tyler's fast asleep. What?" Jacinda frowned and squinted at the clock by the bed. "Of course I know what time it is. Of course this is important! I wouldn't have called if it weren't. No—'' she shook her head vehemently, as if to convince him over the telephone ''—it couldn't wait.''

Dare propped his chin on the heel of one hand and listened. With a grin spreading over his face he settled down to watch a virtuoso in action.

Blowing a tousled curl from her face, in a rush Jacinda blurted out her request. ''Antonia needs a ride. Of course I mean tomorrow.'' Casting a second glance at the clock she amended, ''Okay, so it's today already.'' Silence. ''Naturally I mean on the plane.'' With great innocence, ''Ross, of course with you. Who else?''

Holding the phone from her she grinned at Dare, waiting. After a minute of silence she returned it cautiously to her ear. ''Antonia's going to New York, as you are. No, her flight hasn't been canceled. Why am I asking? Because I'm worried about her. She's tired. The drive to the airport, and then the stop-and-go commercial flights are so hard.'' A second silence, this time longer. ''Why should I think you would murder each other shut up in a small aircraft for hundreds of miles?''

Jacinda caught her lower lip between her teeth and sent Dare an anxious look, but Dare's grin only widened. Most familiar with her delightful wiles, he hadn't a doubt of the outcome.

With a long sigh she moved in for the kill. ''Please, Ross.'' Her voice was softly wistful. ''As a favor to the mother of your godchildren?''

Dare leaned back, his arms folded behind his head, his laughing eyes turned to the ceiling. Ross didn't have a chance.

''No,'' Jacinda drawled the word interminably, letting the wounded sound of it sink in. ''I really don't think I'm being unfair. I wouldn't be unfair. Dare,'' she appealed to her husband's tolerant judgment. ''Would I be unfair?'' Then she said to Ross, ''Dare says I wouldn't.''

Her grin cut short her declaration. ''You will? At six? She'll be there. Remember, no matter what, we love you, Ross.'' The telephone clattered unceremoniously back into its cradle. With a crow of delight Jacinda launched herself across the room and into Dare's waiting arms. "It's going to work. I know it is. When he sees how right this is he'll stop being cross with me."

"Maybe." Dare drew her unresisting body down to his. "First you have to persuade Antonia. I don't think she'll be quite so easy as Ross."

"Why not?"

"Because you don't have her wrapped around your little finger as you do the McLachlans."

"I do?" Jacinda wagged her little finger.

"In spades."

With the lift of a provocative brow, she let her bare breasts brush against his chest. "Even you?"

"Especially me," Dare admitted. "Since the moment I saw you in Atlanta. If there was time I'd show you."

"Show me now."

"What about Antonia?"

"Later," Jacinda murmured as she leaned to his kiss. "I'll talk to Antonia later."

"I don't believe this." Antonia hauled a cosmetic case out of the car, slipping the strap over her shoulder. "I can't believe I let you talk me into this." Eyeing the landing strip where the plane sat, ready and waiting in the early-morning light, she shook her head in wonder. "I've lost my mind. It has to be that. What person in her right mind would let even her best friend talk her into shutting herself up for hours in a flying tin can with a pilot who hates her?"

"It's a nice, respectable, corporate plane, and the pilot doesn't hate you." Jacinda swept up a second bag only to have Dare take it from her.

"He gives a pretty good imitation of it." Antonia hardly noticed that Dare had taken her bag as well, to stow it in the back of the plane. "I can't imagine why I let you talk me into this."

"You're repeating yourself again." Jacinda reminded helpfully.

"I know, but I just can't—" Antonia clamped her teeth on yet another repetition. She protested, but she knew exactly how Jacinda had convinced her to participate in this folly. This dearest and most selfless of friends had come asking a favor with the glow of replete love still shining in her eyes. If agreeing to keep a tired man company on a lonely flight would stop the happy look on Jacinda's face from becoming worry, Antonia would have flown to China with Ross.

"It's time, Antonia."

Ross.

Antonia turned to him as he touched her arm. He'd crossed from the landing strip with Dare, and stood at her shoulder. He wore practical chinos, a rich blue shirt, short desert boots and a worn leather jacket. In his eyes she saw he understood that even for the brittle, self-serving Antonia Russell, saying goodbye to a much-loved friend was never easy.

"I'm sorry." In his face there was compassion. Perhaps in their value of friendships they'd found a rare common ground. "All preflight checks are done. There are changes in the weather that make timing critical. We have to leave. Now."

His goodbyes made the night before, Ross stepped back with a smile for Jacinda and nod to Dare. "Five minutes," he insisted. "I'll wait for you in the plane."

Antonia faced Jacinda, sudden tears springing to her eyes. Then they were holding each other. Laughing and crying and murmuring fond admonitions in this moment that was always hardest.

"Don't stay away so long next time." Releasing Antonia, Jacinda took a step back.

"I won't." Antonia wiped away a tear. "Now that I'm a godmother, I'll be turning up on your doorstep every time you look around. I have to make sure you aren't spoiling my charges."

"Thanks, for everything." Jacinda hesitated again then added, "Especially for this, for today."

Recovering her composure Antonia wagged a finger. "You'll owe me one. And remember, if I don't survive it, I'll be back to haunt you. That's a promise."

"Antonia." Dare touched her arm.

"I know." She turned a sad smile toward him. "Time to go."

Jacinda took comfort in the shelter of Dare's arms as Antonia crossed to the plane. Ross waited in the doorway, watching. He waved to them in the pale morning light and was so like Dare—strong, solid, responsible. She was more convinced than ever this was right.

Ross could give Antonia the love she didn't know she needed. He would take care of her.

Tears threatened again. She couldn't let this beautiful friend walk out of her life for months, perhaps a year, without one special wish. "Antonia!" Jacinda waited until the tall, dark-haired woman turned. "Win an Oscar!"

Antonia laughed. "I intend to."

With one last wave, taking the hand that Ross offered, she disappeared into the plane.

With the newly risen sun at their backs, Dare and Jacinda watched the plane lift off. White and sleek, with the McLachlan logo painted on its wings in the shades of evergreen, it skimmed over the land, rising like a graceful bird above the treetops toward the blue misted mountains on the horizon.

The clamor of the engine had faded when Dare hugged Jacinda, kissing away a tear, teasing a smile to her face. "Your nose is going to grow, Pinocchio."

"You think so?"

"It's a good bet."

"Will you love me anyway?"

"Always, even when your nose is out to here." Dare gestured an impossible distance and kissed her again.

"If it works Ross will forgive me. So will Antonia. If it doesn't, I'll have Antonia's ghost to contend with, won't I?"

"Ross has forgiven you. He sent his love saying he envies Antonia having a friend like you."

"Why didn't he tell me?"

"There was no time. Unstable weather is brewing in the midwest and moving in our direction. He wanted to get in the air and to New York before it arrives. You truly are forgiven. Honey, Ross would forgive you anything."

"Then all I have to worry about is my nose and Antonia's survival."

Dare laughed. "I don't think I'd give either a second thought."

Arm in arm Dare and Jacinda returned to their car, a teasing comment forgotten. Jacinda and Dare were confident that the day would be the first step in bringing happiness like their own to brother and friend.

"Don't!" Ross's voice crackled over the heavy drone of the engine.

Surprised at the unexpected command, Antonia's hand froze in the act of releasing her seat belt. Since settling her in the seat at his side and delivering a minimum of terse instructions Ross had been engrossed in the intricacies of the controls of the plane. Silence lay like a dark wound between them.

More than once Antonia had asked herself why she'd allowed Jacinda to persuade her to be part of this folly. Next, being a realist and realizing that what was begun couldn't be undone, she'd considered suggesting a second truce. Just for the duration of the flight. Just to make the hours ahead of them more bearable. A glimpse at the grim set of his jaw had been enough to discourage that idea. Maybe Jacinda felt that Ross needed company on this flight, but his manner warned he didn't share her belief.

Glumly Antonia had settled down for a long, long flight. She passed the time staring out of the cockpit, ultimately finding fascination in the rise and fall of the forested mountains below. Moving only when she must, she tried to draw as little attention to herself as possible. Evidently her effort had met with smashing success. For the last quarter hour Ross seemed oblivious of her. Until now, when, without looking in her direction, he'd known that she reached for her seat belt.

"Keep your seat belt fastened." His tone was gentler as he turned his gaze from sky. "We could hit turbulence at any time. It's not uncommon to hit a bad patch right about here and not even the wizardry of the autopilot can keep an even keel. Something to do with the way the wind swirls over these mountains." He smiled crookedly at her, a quirk of his lips that left the rest of his face unchanged. "Sorry. The McLachlan company plane isn't quite what you're accustomed to. Makes for a rougher flight under the best of conditions. So, humor me, if you will. Anyway, we wouldn't want a sudden downdraft to toss you around the cabin and blacken one of your gorgeous eyes, would we? You'd have a helluva time explaining that to your adoring fans, wouldn't you?"

Antonia felt the subtle cut of sarcasm. A sense of the hopelessness of their never-ending battle settled like a shadow over the day and pain she didn't understand clogged her throat. As she'd had no response to a cynical salute made across a crowded room, she had none now and simply turned away. With only a nod that she understood, she moved her hands from the belt, folding them obediently in her lap.

Ross stared at her, taken by surprise by her easy compliance. He expected the fiery rhetoric that marked their encounters. When she focused her attention once more on the landscape, he let his gaze wander over her. As if it had gotten easier with practice, he found himself admitting again how extraordinarily beautiful she was. Her features were even and, totally devoid of makeup, almost delicate. Bare, her skin was a natural golden-tan. Her hair, that glorious sable mane, was smoothed back from her forehead and tied with a ribbon that matched her shirt. On her lips the color was repeated, but there was none of the toughness he'd come to expect in their pensive curve. Her jacket and slacks were of a soft tan fabric, designed for elegance, but sturdy in the bargain. Her shoes were hand-stitched desert boots, new and stiff and shiny.

Except for a purple scarf folded charmingly as an ascot tucked into the deep closure of her shirt, and ridiculously long fingernails that echoed again the ribbon in her hair, she could have been any sophisticated, no-nonsense traveler headed to Anywhere, USA.

She could have been, but she wasn't.

For reasons he didn't understand, her poised and amiable common sense annoyed him. His lips thinned to a grim line, his eyes narrowed, challenging the veneer, searching for the artifice he hated, finding not even a shred. After a long while he looked away. Staring stonily into the empty sky he tried to empty his mind of her as well.

The sun moved toward the meridian. The day stretched smoothly into eternity. The engine droned steadily onward. No downdrafts nor crosscurrents pummeled them. Clouds gathered on the horizon lay quiet and innocuous for now.

The plane literally flew itself. Unengaged and unoccupied, Ross sighed heavily, and defeated, found his gaze drawn back to her.

Dear heaven how she intrigued him, and puzzled him. But, if he were honest, his reaction to her was most puzzling. He liked women. Tall, short, fat, skinny, young, old, attached or unattached, he liked and respected them. It was quite simply an innate part of his personality. A fact that both he and women he knew understood and accepted. A mutual admiration, more often platonic than not. The rapport it created influenced the choice of his specialty in medicine almost as much as his fondness for children. This accord shared with the mothers of his young patients contributed mightily to a thriving pediatric practice.

Away from his work, away from his brothers, in the long quiet hours spent tramping alone through the forest, or wading a trout stream, he'd reflected that perhaps he liked women too well. Though he'd watched, applauded, and sometimes schemed, as Dare tumbled into love with Jacinda, in reaching the great, good age of thirty-three Ross liked many woman yet loved none.

He hadn't loved, but he'd never been hostile. Never before Antonia. From their first glance, their first word, dislike tangled around them like a bitter vine bearing fruits of ridicule and contempt.

Why? He'd asked himself but found no good answer.

Differences of values?

Differences of choices?

But none that were intolerable or unforgivable within the bounds of normal acquaintance. What logical reason could he give to deep-seated hostility that made no sense?

And, dammit, why did it have to make sense anyway? he wondered irritably.

A maverick wind pummeled the small plane, riveting Ross's attention on fluttering gauges and meters. His hand grasped the controls, ready to take command if need be. If human judgments were needed. A muffled gasp, suppressed almost before it was uttered, was Antonia's only reaction as she reeled in her seat.

"Crosswind," he explained tersely. "Happens all the time. You wouldn't notice in an airliner."

Too busy keeping herself upright to care if the last was intended as another sarcasm, Antonia nodded, relying on his phenomenal peripheral vision to catch the minute motion.

"There's bad weather ahead, but not for a while." Thoughts diverted, his irritation eased, his mood mellowed. "This is only a little warning. Just sit tight, we'll be out of it soon." He flashed her a reassuring smile. A complete smile that crinkled his eyes and softened the stern lines that bracketed his mouth. "You'll be safe and sound on the ground in New York before the worst of what's brewing breaks."

"How do you know?" Antonia muttered through teeth still clenched against a cry.

"An excellent weather service, a more than excellent plane and a head start." The smile again, rare, natural and without a trace of mockery. "With that bit of help, I'll take care of you. Jacinda would never forgive me if I didn't."

"I'm not sure I would, either," Antonia quipped and, as the turbulence quieted, loosened her death grip on her seat.

Ross grinned and concentrated on his flying. Antonia was sitting with her head back against the seat, her eyes closed, exhausted from the tension. When he was finally satisfied there were no more maverick currents sweeping before the storm and tranquility restored, his mind turned, as if it were a magnet, to the woman at his side. To differences and tolerance.

But he had no forgiveness for Antonia's differences. No tolerance. He could find no saving grace in her. No, in fairness he corrected himself, he hadn't *allowed* himself to recognize any saving grace before this visit.

Turning his head only a bit to catch a better view of her, he wondered why this time? Where did the difference lie? In him? In Antonia?

As the sun continued to rise and the morning paled with its light, he studied her, seeking his answers. In profile against the backdrop of the empty sky she seemed smaller. Her features, in repose, were less flamboyant. As she stared into the distance, there was a softness about her. Ross had the uncanny feeling that in this quiet woman he was seeing an Antonia few knew. The woman perhaps only Jacinda understood.

Who among her loyal fans would equate the glamorous celebrity with the struggling actress that, in her climb to stardom, never forgot a friend? Who knew of the interrupted journeys to exotic locations, of the impromptu detours, all to steal only an hour or two with that friend? Who but Jacinda's close-knit circle had been privileged to see a star, out of her element, accepting the responsibility of the spiritual guidance of not just one child but two?

Few had seen. Few would believe. Not even himself, until he watched as she quieted a baby with clumsy tenderness.

Antonia Russell. A star. A woman. One he'd never really known.

Ross turned away, bringing his attention back to the clouds that were beginning to move. Climbing too soon like dark towers over the rim where the earth met the sky. Had anything so magnificent ever been so capricious? he wondered. Or so lethal?

A seed of worry began to take root. He checked the autopilot and scanned the gauges. Perfect. Everything was perfect, but for how long? An involuntary tremor coursed through his body and forboding lay like lead in his gut.

Ross was a man of the country, but no fool, and perhaps more in touch with himself than most. He recognized his own competence as a pilot and appreciated it. He was a natural and better than average—far better. The definitive factor, he knew, was instinct. Right now his instinct was keening like a bowstring. Yet there was nothing to see, nothing to do. The storm was hours away, they were miles ahead of it. However, there was something. Omen, premonition, or simply a harbinger of a waiting storm? All Ross could do was wait for whatever was coming.

He leveled another long, hard look at the control panel, as if the answers were hidden there. Their readings were normal. Nothing was amiss, except in that nether region of the mind that sensed and felt what it couldn't see.

The sky above and below was as clear and bright as ever, but at the core of reason Ross felt the insidious nag of apprehension. Enough that he would have considered turning back were it nor for his race with the storm. Turning back meant their path would dissect the projected path of a line of squalls. Praying the weather service lived up to its good name, he grimly kept himself from setting a new course.

Time lay heavy on him, turning mind and body increasingly restless. The air in the cabin seemed charged, the tension so thick, surely Antonia with an actress's creative perception must feel it, too.

Turning his head to reassure her, his heart lurched when he saw that her head was bowed and tears sparkled on her lashes. "Hey!" It was a measure of how on edge he was that he touched her cheek without realizing that he had until he felt the smooth satin of her skin. For a split second he wondered if it was her malaise he felt. Letting the backs of his fingers trail to her chin, he tilted her face toward his. "What's this?"

"Nothing." Antonia blinked and cleared her throat of its whispery huskiness. She tried to turn her head away, but the swift curving of his palm at her jaw denied her even that little privacy.

"Nothing?" he asked softly, his thumb moving slowly against the tender flesh of the top of her throat.

"A mood," she muttered, desperate to turn away from the scrutiny of his scintillating gaze. With a deprecating gesture and an unconvincing laugh she added, "The actresses' mercuric temperament, remember? You've run afoul of it recent enough."

Ross considered the near panic he'd seen after the christening, and now the tears, and dismissed her excuse. Antonia Russell was far too strong to let moods rule her life. Perhaps this unsettling atmosphere had precipitated her anxiety, but something more than temperament was disturbing her.

The same intuition that had every nerve ending standing at attention had him saying, "It's all right, Antonia. There's no one here to see, no one to care if you aren't perfect. Even a glamorous, successful woman can have doubts and fears. She can be tired. She can feel lonely and sad and even a little lost when she's left the friend who means most to her in all the world. Especially when she has no idea when they'll meet again."

With the ridge of his thumb he traced the line of her jaw, stroking skin that was marvelous. Perhaps it was the jittery, skittish feeling that still held him in its grip that gave him an almost clairvoyant understanding of her distress. Perhaps it was that clairvoyance that made him want to lift her into his lap and hold her. Or perhaps it was that by nature and profession he was a comforter, healer of psyche as well as body.

But, he reminded himself, this was Antonia, not one of his small charges, and a plane wasn't the place for what he was thinking. In no more than a whisper he offered the little solace he could. "It's all right to miss Jacinda, and it's all right to cry. Tears won't make you one bit less a star." His voice dropped lower, quieter still. "I promise."

"Don't!" Antonia closed her eyes, shutting his image from her sight but never her mind. "Don't be kind."

"Me? Kind?" He laughed softly. "To you? Never!"

Antonia's lashes lifted, her gray eyes focused slowly on his face then lowered to his mouth. "I think you are." Her expression was grave, her gaze earnest. "I think you're really very kind. And now... by understanding how much Jacinda means to me and caring that it hurts to leave her... even to me."

Ross's laugh faded, surprise leaped into his eyes. He drew a deep breath and then another. "We seem to have another first." He busied himself tucking a stray curl behind her ear with great care. "For once we've both looked beneath the surface, and maybe what we've seen isn't so bad."

"Maybe." Her eyes glittered with remembered tears.

Ross shrugged aside the qualification. "That's a start."

Antonia never had the chance to ask a start for what.

An explosive jolt shuddered through the plane, pinning her to her seat as if they were suddenly tumbling through space. A scream was ripped unuttered from her throat and her stomach lurched against her ribs as the nose of the plane plunged downward. Caught in the eddy of winds packing the punch of a tornado they were sucked toward the earth in a vortex at speeds that would surely destroy them.

As if everything was etched into her mind, she was aware of minute detail. Of wildly oscillating gauges, the pressure, the scream of smoking engines. Ross's grave expression beneath a sheen of sweat. The taut strain of tendons. The bulge of muscles in his shoulders and arms as he battled the shuddering plane.

Antonia's head was splitting, her eyes stung, her vision blurred. They were falling at incredible speeds but the pull of gravity turned Ross's every move to slow motion. His features were flattened against his skull, his lips drawn back in a rictus. With a guttural scream rising from the bottom of his lungs, he nearly stood as he leaned all his weight to the fight. The plane shuddered again, fighting against itself, against Ross, against the elements. The nose rose a fraction, then dipped, then rose again. Then, suddenly, the sound and pressure eased, the bucking stopped. The steel edged tension in Ross dropped away as arms that were bone and sinew and trembling, knotted power relaxed.

They were free.

In an eerie quiet the plane righted. At little higher than the treetops they were gliding in a level path.

"Go to the back of the cockpit, Antonia. Strap yourself in the middle seat. As tightly as you can. Put your head down, cover your face." His voice rang hollowly in the void, a monotone delivering a desperate recitation. "And if you know any prayers, say them." Without looking at her he reached over and flipped open her seat belt.

"Ross, what—"

"Dammit! Do as I say!" he commanded gutturally.

"But—"

"For God's sake, Antonia, just do it! We're going down."

Then she understood the utter quiet. The engines were gone. Destroyed in that shrieking, diving battle. Stripped and bent and mangled they were useless derelicts. The plane was without power and was losing the little altitude it had left.

Antonia lurched to her feet then hesitated. As if he read her mind, Ross looked up. "There's nothing you can do to help."

For a second that seemed a millennium she stared down at him seeing a man she'd never seen. A man she didn't want to lose.

"We're running out of time, Antonia."

When she gestured, entreating him to seek protection with her, he shook his head, only the barest move, his eyes never leaving hers. "Go."

Still she stood, feeling the floor tremble beneath her feet as the plane faltered.

"Please," Ross murmured.

Antonia drew a deep rasping breath, trying to still the shaking that sapped her will. Then without thinking she nodded, her mind a blank but for Ross's plea. Yet when she would have turned obediently, he lifted a hand, staying her, waiting.

When her palm met his, his fingers closed, capturing hers. "Stay with the wreckage." The plane shook as if trying to rid itself of its skin. "If I'm not with you, stay as near as you can. No matter how long it takes, Dare will find you." Mountains loomed before them. The last hope was gone. "Be safe." His fingers tightened before he gave her a little shove.

There was no time to see if she obeyed as he turned and trees rose up to meet them.

Four

Treetops battered the undercarriage. A wing dipped, the tail veered violently. Thrown as much as stumbling to the seat Ross indicated, Antonia fumbled with her seat belt. As it clicked into place the sheer rock face of a mountain loomed stark and unmerciful before them. A bitten lip sealed her outcry. Nothing muted the terror resounding in her brain in a never-ending echo.

Her breath stopped in bursting lungs and with it she was sure her faltering heart. As the mountain filled her vision a part of her remained detached from the horror, watching in slow motion things that happened too fast for mind and body to comprehend.

This shouldn't be happening, yet it was. A storm threatened on the horizon, not here. But in a mad little world, beneath a pristine sky, a whim of the wind sent a plane streaking toward towering gray cliffs as a thing demented.

There was no escape. No hope. In despair, in resignation, accepting the inevitable Antonia bent at the waist, her forehead touching her knees. The image she took with her, graven in that awful darkness of waiting, was of Ross.

The cockpit quivered and lurched. The nose lifted, the tail plummeted, giving the sense of falling backward before leveling off.

Ross, Antonia knew without thinking, fighting to keep them aloft. A battle he could not win. The stalled engines would not respond. The aircraft was finished with flying. With her eyes squeezed shut, wrapping her arms around her legs, Antonia braced for the final horror.

But the horror was not to be swift, the deadly implosion of head-on collision of stone and machine did not come. Instead, the plane flopped like an ungainly whale on dry land. Then they were on nearly level terrain. Careening out of control, but level, thank God. The scream of tearing metal was almost human as the landing gear broke off, and with it wheels and struts. Then the earth was clawing at the belly of this fallen intruder, peeling it away layer after layer. The floor erupted beneath her feet, and the screams of the dying plane, coupled now with her own, grew louder.

Incredibly the lunatic skidding decelerated. The impact of a wing plowing into the ground then ripping away set them spinning on an imaginary axis. Centrifugal force sent Antonia flying against the seat. She tried to pull away but her hair was caught in torn metal. For one millisecond she was held prisoner and in the next brutally ripped free by the motion of the tumbling plane. Her vision blurred, her face throbbed. Dimly, half conscious, she heard her voice call his name.

Then, blessedly, even that little window of lucidity slammed shut.

Antonia felt herself being pulled down into a dark void that grew darker, and darker still. Until there was nothing.

First there was silence. Then the rasp of a ragged breath and the slow, regular pound of distant thunder.

No! Not thunder. A heartbeat. Her heart.

She was alive!

Antonia's eyes swept open.

Nothing.

She saw nothing. Only a nebulous gray cloud that hovered over her face. Her mind struggled through a cocoon of confusion. She blinked her stinging eyes, trying to force them to focus. Almost idly she thought of her glasses, those silly, dainty concoctions she wore perched on the end of her nose when she read scripts or menus. As she rallied the will to reach for them, the cloud moved. Moved, but did not dissipate. She tried again, squinting, narrowing her field of vision. The cloud became a strip of cloth swaying like a hypnotist's amulet before her face.

Not cloth. Leather. Torn from the interior of the plane.

Reality did not come gradually, nor gently.

"Ross!" Antonia struggled to rise as appalling memories ravaged her. "Ross!" An unseen hand held her. In her frenzy jagged metal scraped her shoulder and ripped her blouse. Pain served like a slap to calm her. The threat of hysteria ebbed.

Antonia lay back, concentrating on what she knew, what she understood. She was lying on her side. Her seat had been ripped from its braces and she with it. The back was mangled and the arm, but the seat was intact. It was only the seat belt, its buckle still fastened securely, that held her.

With unsteady hands she unbuckled it. Her attempt to rise was as unsuccessful as the first. Her muscles hadn't the strength. On her hands and knees she crawled through the debris. Grasping the back of Ross's seat, she dragged herself to her feet. When she saw him a scream rose from the depths of her despair.

"Ross!" In a surge of renewed strength she scrambled over wreckage to him. He sat, still and lifeless, his head thrown back against the seat. With trembling fingers she touched the pulse beneath his ear. Her knees buckled, and only a hand flung out at the rubble that had been her first seat kept her from falling. His flesh was warm to her touch, his pulse was weak but steady.

For a brief, joyful moment, Antonia wanted to gather him in her arms. They were alive...*she* was alive...because of him. She wanted to hold him, to celebrate this gift he'd given, but she dared not.

"God help me, what do I do?" Feverishly she searched her memory, cursing the little medical knowledge she had. Question after question tumbled through a mind dazed by shock, struggling desperately to remain calm and rational. Rubbing her aching temple with a shaking hand she tried to think. She couldn't just leave him as he was, but would it hurt to move him? What damage might she do? A grim smile lined her drawn face as she wondered how many survived such crises as this, only to fall victim of would-be rescuers.

"Ross." She touched his shoulder, careful not to shake him. "Please tell me what to do."

Ross stirred and moaned, then was silent.

Antonia backed away, denying tears that threatened. Sinking to her knees, she buried her face in her hands. She wanted nothing more than to cover her head and curl into a ball and sleep. When she woke up this would all be a dream. The crash would never have happened. Ross would look up from the controls, a wicked grin and a taunt on his lips.

It wasn't a dream. It wouldn't be no matter how long she hid from it. This was real. This was life, the life Ross had given her. By all that was holy, she would do the same for him.

Her heart pounded, her mouth was dry, she was more afraid than she'd ever been as she climbed to her feet. Anger and adrenaline became the source of her strength. Demanding of herself that she think logically and ignoring the pain in her head, she took stock of their circumstance.

She'd had no concept of the crash site. Nothing in her life prepared her for the complete ruin. Both wings were gone and half the tail section. Through the ruptured floor she could see the ground. Behind this broken shell that resembled nothing as much as a bale of scrap metal, lay a scattered trail of unrecognizable debris.

The plane had skidded across the mountaintop and come to rest in a clearing. But where were they really? Clinging to a precarious ledge? Perched on the edge of a chasm?

She had to know. Before she could make any move to help Ross, she had to understand what she was dealing with, where she was going. Allowing herself one touch of the back of her hand against his cheek, assuring that its living warmth was not a waking dream, she clambered down though the rift in the floor and dropped to the ground.

Straightening from a half crouch, she stood stock still. "Oh, my Lord," she muttered. Then striding to the end of the clearing, at the edge of a vertical drop she stopped, turning in a half circle. Hardly believing her eyes, she looked out from what seemed like the top of the world. For as far as she could see there were peaks and valleys. One flowed into the next, and the next, and the next, until she could see no more. Each, God help them, was densely forested and as barren of civilized life as the one before it.

"A wilderness," she muttered dispirited. "A mountain wilderness, where no man has ever been, or will ever come."

Spinning away from the sprawling, frightening view, she concentrated on the little patch of rock-strewn clearing. Rocks? Another time she would have mocked the misnomer. They were boulders, dammit. Half as big as the plane itself. Stubby pines sprang from their midst, some broken and twisted, some sheared cleanly in half. The nose of the plane, or what was left of it, tilted squarely on top of what looked to be a wall of stone.

"A wall?" Antonia laughed suddenly and began to run. A wall meant people. People meant help for Ross.

Falling on her knees before it, running her hands over it, her laughter died. There was no denying it was a wall, but crumbling and ancient, and with little mortar. For whatever reason this line of stone had been laid, it was never meant to be more than temporary. Constructed, perhaps, in passing by a trapper or explorer long since in his grave.

Kneeling on dry grass, her fingers linked at her thighs, Antonia faced the truth. There would be no help for them. What had to be done, she must do. Climbing to her feet, with her fists clenched she looked out again at the desolation. The terror of the death throes of a tortured plane was nothing like the terror of silence. Antonia understood loneliness, but she had never been so alone.

A rising wind moved over the clearing, rippling tall grass, moaning through the skeletal remains of what was once a plane, bringing with it the reek of oil. Though it seemed like forever, she had spent only minutes exploring the clearing. Now the thickening stench of spilling fuel warned even that precious little time had run out.

The feel of rain was in the air. Distant clouds were not so distant anymore. Building and blackening, they had begun to move, bringing with them lightning that would seek high ground. There was no longer right or wrong for Ross. With the threat of lightning and its fire, there was no choice. She had to move him. Away from the plane. Away from harm. A sliver of metal hummed like a tuning fork. From somewhere inside the cockpit something dislodged and fell with a clatter. Antonia's shirt was plastered to her body by a quickening gust. The storm was not imminent, but it was coming, and there was much she must do.

Her eyes were dry as she walked back to the wreckage. She was done with any hint of tears and with dreams of help. Ross had done his part keeping them alive this far. Now it was her turn to see that his efforts weren't wasted.

Reaching over her head, she grasped a bar and then another. For a moment she stared through the jagged opening into the cockpit. Ross needed her. No one had ever truly needed her until now. The thought sent a strange shiver of sensation through her. Fear? Yes, of more than she could comprehend. But something else as well. Something she'd never felt before. Something too nebulous to name.

Confused and weary, Antonia leaned her head against her arm. She reflected on her life and was surprised that she thought most of the loneliness. Of one hectic day sliding into another, with no one who really mattered beside her. No one who wanted her, who needed her. Without realizing it, she had been alone even then.

Is that what it meant to be needed, she wondered, never having to be alone?

Her mind was a bruised morass. Too much had happened too rapidly. She couldn't deal with it. And, at the moment, there were more important things than her troubled thoughts. Grimly, setting everything aside, Antonia lifted herself into the plane.

"Ross. Can you hear me?" Antonia leaned over him, touching him. His pulse was stronger now and steadier. His color was better. The swelling at the side of his face was beginning to discolor. There were rusty stains of blood on his shirt, but when she looked for cuts and abrasions she found none. Mystified, but grateful, she dismissed them.

"...toni..."

A nuance, less than a whisper, so low that at first she was afraid she'd imagined it, or that she'd wished it. Crouching down beside him, she saw that his eyes were open. Dazed and unfocused, they were still the most beautiful sight she'd ever seen. Closing her fingers over his wrist, feeling the life pulse there, she said more calmly than she felt, "I'm here."

"What..." He moistened parched lips, searching for words.

"The plane lost power," she explained, not burdening him with more than his disoriented mind could deal with.

"Crash!" The word was surprisingly clear in its urgency.

"Yes," she confirmed as calmly as before. "At the crest of a mountain rather than into it, thanks to you."

"Hur...hur...?" He frowned, his eyes closing again as he tried to concentrate.

"You banged your head. You've been unconscious."

He made an impatient gesture with his head that drained the little returning color from his face. In a visible effort he strained to regain his scattered thoughts. "Are you...?" Beads of sweat glistened on his forehead. The effort was too much.

Removing the scarf that dangled haphazardly at her neck, Antonia wiped his brow. "I'm not hurt. A little bruised around the edges, but considering the circumstances, I'm in great shape." Without thinking she stuffed the scarf into her shirt and leaned closer, and in her best sexy voice, the voice that always struck sparks between them, she murmured, "Since you wouldn't know a great shape if you saw it, Doc, I'll have no comments from you."

Ross made a dry coughing sound, and incredibly, Antonia realized he was trying to laugh. "Wouldn't—" he flinched and she saw how much the attempt cost him, yet determinedly he continued "—wouldn't dare."

At this sign of the old Ross, Antonia felt her spirits rise. Things couldn't be all bad if he could muster the strength for their game. Thunder had begun to tumble through the passes and over the faraway mountain, the sound of it carried on intensifying gusts. Time had become critical. What she must do would be hard for her but harder for Ross. Perhaps a shield of banter would distract and ease their way.

"You don't fool me, handsome." She brushed a lock of hair from his poor battered forehead. "You're only being kind to me because I have you at my mercy."

"Some..." He took a deep breath and his eyes cleared a bit. "Something like that."

His speech was still halting, but clearer. Antonia knew it was another measure of the power of his determination. "Considering that this is a rare opportunity, I have more planned for you."

"Sus—" a pause as he thought his way through what he meant to say "—suspected as much."

"Ross." Antonia's face was solemn, her hands were clasped in a punishing grip. "We have to get out of the plane. The weather that was predicted has changed course. It's coming our way. I know there's little chance that lightning will strike here, but if it should..."

"Fuel."

"Yes." As adrenaline had bolstered her strength, it served now to clear his thoughts. But for how long? she wondered. "The tanks are ruptured, Ross. We could go up like firecrackers on the Fourth of July."

"Firecrackers?" His lifted brow was truly the old Ross.

"Big ones." She grinned before she realized that she had. It was hardly a time for laughter. Or was it? When things looked beyond redemption, could laughter be the beginning of hope?

"Time to go?"

"Yeah." Antonia watched as he struggled with his seat belt, but his hands wouldn't seem to work. Brushing them gently aside, only a little more steadily she dealt with buckles and straps. When he started to rise, her hand on his shoulder stopped him. "Let me help."

With a shake of his head he tried to stand. His legs refused him. Grim and shaking, a muscle flickering in his jaw, he tried again. With a mighty effort he managed, swaying as if he were a newborn colt, before collapsing in his seat. The odor of fuel was almost suffocating now. His face was gray and streaked with sweat as he looked up at her. He smiled crookedly, a strong man whose strength had betrayed him, and in his eyes the knowledge of what he must ask of her.

"Maybe..." he said softly, haltingly, "maybe I will, after all."

Passing a weary arm over her forehead, Antonia surveyed the results of her labor. She had made trip after trip into the plane, bringing with her whatever she thought would be of use. Her head was aching in earnest now, but she hadn't the time to think of it. With a glance at the massive overhang of rock where Ross lay sleeping or unconscious on a bed made of clothing from their suitcases, she began her last trek to the wreckage.

As fumes seared the raw tissues of her nose and throat and blinded her burning eyes with tears, she groped her way through the metal shell. Almost by luck her hand brushed over the soft fur coat she'd discarded as useless earlier. It was neither folly nor vanity that had her venturing again into danger to retrieve it now.

As the day had gone on the temperature had dropped drastically and the night promised to be even colder. With the wind and the ever widening circle of spilled fuel, she dared not risk a fire.

The black mink was heavy as sin and as warm as hell. Ross wouldn't be cold.

"Antonia?"

Her feet had barely touched the ground beneath the cockpit when she heard him call. The heavy mink flung carelessly over one shoulder she hurried to their cavelike shelter. Kneeling at his side she stroked his cheek, repeating an already familiar litany, "I'm here, Ross."

His eyes opened, his head turned slowly, his gaze finding her. "Where were you?"

"There were supplies in the plane I thought we might need."

"Oh." He frowned and nodded as if reminded of something he shouldn't have forgotten. "Of course." He lifted himself from his prone position, half sitting, half leaning against the boulder at his back. "I should help."

"No." Antonia laid a restraining hand against his chest. "There's no need. Everything's done." At least everything she knew to do.

Ross nodded and closed his eyes, then abruptly roused again. "Concussion," he said clearly, touching the side of his head and the swollen brow, as if on another level his bruised brain functioned and diagnosed instinctively. His eyelids fluttered. "How did I get here?"

Though his speech was clear, there was confusion in his face. The look of a man who understood the reality of what had happened, yet couldn't quite grasp it. Antonia was glad he didn't remember their retreat from the plane. The nightmare of stumbling and falling, his arm around her shoulder, his weight bearing her down with him. Of climbing, painfully, with her, first to their knees, then to their feet, only to fall again.

Their progress to this overhang she'd chosen for their refuge had been clumsy and painful. It was best that it remain forgotten. "You're here now." Realizing that her hand still rested against his chest, she moved it away. "That's all that matters."

Ross didn't agree, but the dizziness that gnawed constantly at the edge of his mind blotted out his thoughts.

Crouching as she was, Antonia watched and worried. His stuporous sleep was abnormal. She knew little of concussions, but prayed he was right, that it was only that. When she thought of the destroyed hulk that lay in the clearing, the miracle was that he had no other apparent injury. For that matter, beyond some bruises, some strained and sore muscles, and an aching cheek neither had she.

While Ross slept the wind howled over the mountain and through the trees, but within the circle of stone they were sheltered from the brunt of it. The sky had grown dark. Churning black clouds lay so low she wondered if she could reach out and touch them. Thunder rumbled, lightning flashed; it seemed instead as if its fury reached down for her.

Shivering, she reached for the coat flung carelessly on the ground. Turning to Ross, intending to cover him with it, she found him watching her. In this rare moment his eyes were clear, and lucid. He smiled, a lopsided quirk of his mouth, but a smile that said he understood her fear of the storm. The hand he lifted to her was steady. When his fingers twined in her hair, drawing her down to the bed she'd made him, she went willingly.

His arms held her close, her head lay on his chest. Warmed by black mink and with the rhythm of his heart to soothe her, Antonia found herself succumbing to fatigue.

"No!" She struggled to sit up, afraid to sleep. Afraid that if she did, Ross would drift away from her.

"I'm tired, Antonia."

She listened mutely. He said it as a matter of fact, but his voice had thickened. From the need of rest or from injury?

His hand rested lightly on her shoulder. "There's nothing we can do but ride out the storm." With only token pressure he drew her down to him again. "Nothing we can do but wait..." He didn't complete his thought as he rested his cheek against her hair.

There was no need, Antonia knew he was speaking of himself, of an injury that might be as simple as a concussion, or perhaps not so simple.

"Sleep." Beneath the rumble of thunder his voice was soft, seductive. "Until the storm is finished." Then as if he understood what frightened her more than the wrath of the elements, he murmured, "I won't leave you." He stroked her back, soothing her. When she relaxed completely against him, he whispered, "I promise."

"My name is Ross McLachlan."

At the sound of his own voice Ross opened his eyes. There was pain from the light, but not the throbbing agony that threatened his sanity before.

When before? he wondered, and realized he didn't know.

He closed his eyes. Fragments of memory teased at him, then slipped away before he could weave them together. An ice pick stabbed at his brain, but its point had been dulled by rote. Where was he? And why did it seem so important that he remember his name?

The scent of wood smoke tickled his nose, but it was a drift of moss and wild roses that haunted him.

His mind was a blank, the last thing he remembered was reaching down for Antonia, to help her into the plane.

"Antonia?" He bolted upright and for an instant thought he'd ripped his head from his shoulders. Then as the pain burrowed viciously into his skull obliterating all but intolerable agony, he wished he had. When he could see more than the bright spots dancing before his eyes, the scene that greeted him was bizarre. Like some heathen sybarite he was draped with a jumble of colorful silks and furs.

No, not furs. Fur. Black mink to be exact. He couldn't remember what he'd just been thinking, but he hadn't any trouble remembering that he'd last seen the coat draping Antonia's beautiful body, not his own.

So much for long-term memory. Short-term presented the problem. But why was Antonia so much on his mind? And why in hell was he lying here decorated like a Christmas tree?

Climbing to his feet one cautious inch at a time, he divested himself of one last clinging wisp of silk and refused to wonder what it was or why it was there. Ignoring his head and wobbly legs, he shuffled between the stones to the clearing. He stopped, reaching out for a nearby stone to keep from falling, sickness rising from deep inside him.

"Oh, hell," he whispered, sure he had gone mad. He blinked his eyes, willing back his sanity, willing the nightmare away. But when he looked again nothing had changed.

The meadow was a battle zone. The plane, *his* plane, was torn and twisted. Only the McLachlan logo, oddly intact, made it recognizable as what it had been. Ross stared at the stylized evergreen that shone like an emerald in sunlight. No one could have escaped from the heap of scrap alive. He swayed on his feet and was reminded that he was exquisitely alive.

Before his blank stare an image flickered like a broken loop of film. Antonia taking his hand. Over and over, Antonia boarding the plane.

The plane that lay in the clearing. "Oh, dear God! No!"

Ross began to run. Her name, a cry torn again and again from his lips, echoed through an empty ruin. Then her arms were around him, holding him, her voice soothing.

Antonia. He stared at her. He had to be mad.

"I'm here, Ross." Standing in the shadow of the ruin she held him until his panic subsided. Her face was flushed, her hair disheveled from her race across the clearing. Her shirt was plastered to her from the cup of water she'd sent flying when she heard his cry. "I'm fine." She gripped his arms. As she had so many times in days past, she assured him, "I'm truly all right."

Ross backed away, but not beyond her touch. He wasn't sure he could believe his eyes, or his ears. He touched her cheek, feeling the warmth of her. She wasn't a figment from his missing short-term memory.

His gaze riveted on her face. He remembered perfection. "What?" His fingers hovered at her temple, then fell away. His voice was hoarse with distress. "What happened to your face?"

"It's just a scratch." Antonia dismissed the jagged wound. She'd been aware only of a dull ache in her head, until he'd first asked. She'd lost count of the number of times now. As he'd drifted in and out of awareness, he'd become obsessed by it.

"It's more than a scratch." A frown drew harsh lines in his gaunt face.

"It doesn't matter." Though there was a mirror in her luggage, she hadn't looked. She didn't want to. In the days when she thought Ross might die, it hadn't mattered. Now that he was standing before her, weak, but lucid, it still didn't.

Ross's stare raked over the plane, then turned again to her. "I thought you were..."

"I know." Antonia stopped his words with her fingers. "I'm sorry, I didn't mean to frighten you. I had gone for water. There's a seep on the other side of the clearing. The water's clean and cool. In your delirium you've asked for water."

His eyes went to the plane again, as if he couldn't believe that either of them had survived. Given his condition, he was just beginning to understand the magnitude of what she'd done. "How long?"

"Three days."

"Concussion?"

"Yes. At times you were lucid. You understood what was wrong and told me what to expect. What to do. Then you said and did things you wouldn't remember."

"A storm. I remember a storm."

Antonia linked her fingers through his. "Come with me back to camp and I'll tell you everything."

For the first time in days she felt a glimmer of hope.

"You believed me?"

"Yes." Antonia ceased combing her hair for a moment and met his incredulous gaze levelly. "Because you promised."

"I promised!"

"Because you wouldn't lie to me." Antonia continued as if he hadn't interrupted.

Ross was unable, or unwilling to comprehend the sort of trust that allowed Antonia to believe a promise made in delirium. His promise that he wouldn't leave her, a pledge that he would live. He had no idea what he was saying then, he had no memory of it now. Yet she believed. And believing became her talisman as she watched over him.

The wisdom she had shown in assessing their predicament and in choosing a campsite was astonishing. The superhuman effort needed to get him from the plane defied comprehension. The courage it took to return time and again, stripping the plane of all they might need? Ross hadn't the words for it.

And the silly, extravagant mink, representative of their differences had been a godsend against the cold when a fire would have meant their lives.

Though she'd told the story over and over throughout the day, until she was weary with the telling, Ross knew there was more. More than he could reckon. More, he was sure than she would ever say. The private things she would never discuss.

When he took stock he found he was unshaven, but clean. His clothing was fresh, and warm. He was shaky but not pitifully weak. After the rain and with the passage of time, Antonia dared risk a fire and had contrived to make a broth of sorts of the food she scrounged from their supplies. Ross had a vague recollection of a cup held to his lips.

Now, as he watched her over a camp fire and listened, he had trouble believing this was the glamorous Antonia Russell. His nemesis, who had only to breathe the same air as he for slings and arrows to fly.

She was still magnificent, in the dancing light her hair slipped through the comb in a dark cloud. Her cleanly scrubbed face, without the artifice was like the palest, translucent amber. The shadows beneath her eyes suggested that while he slept and recuperated she stood guard.

He didn't ask, for he knew she would deny what her slender body told him—that he had been given the lion's share of their meager food. This from the selfish prima donna whose one saving grace was her loyalty to Jacinda? Which was she? The glittering star beyond the reach of mortal man, or the woman sitting cross-legged in the dust, watching him over the blaze of their campfire?

Ross realized he was staring and looked away, choosing another subject. "You saw no sign of search planes?"

"There were planes, but none came close. I can't be certain if they were searching for us." Antonia laid aside her comb, defeated by a tangle that wouldn't budge. She didn't care, it had only been busywork to avoid the intensity of his stare.

"Dare will search every corner of the world if he must."

"I know." Next Antonia took up her brush. Dare would search, but would he find them? To hide her misgivings she returned her attention to her hair, giving the impossible snarl another try.

"We'll give him one more day, then we'll start down the mountain."

With the brush still caught in her hair, she looked up, surprise shining in her eyes. In an isolated flash of memory, Ross heard himself cautioning that if he were not with her, she must stay with the plane. He waited for her protest, instead she said, "You think it's wiser to move rather than wait?"

"Yes." He could have told her it was wisest because there was little food left. Or that, though it was spring, at this elevation the nights were bitterly cold and would gradually sap her strength. Or that March was a capricious month. The month that brought spring flowers one day, and the deepest snows of the year the next.

He could have told her all those things, but he didn't. Instead he banked the fire, lining it more heavily with small stones to absorb the heat. With a nod to the tangle of silk and fur that had been their bed, he said, "It's only a little past dusk, but we should turn in. We're both exhausted, and tomorrow will be a busy day."

Antonia's mouth was suddenly dry. She couldn't look at him as he stood, towering over her. When he was ill and needed her, it had seemed natural to sleep with him in the makeshift bed, holding him and being held. Now that he was alert and recovering, the necessary arrangement was intolerable. The cold and their meager covering made any alternative impossible. What she couldn't avoid, she chose to delay. At least for a while. "You go. I have some things to do. I'll be there later."

Ross stared down at her bent head, wondering what urgent chore she must do. Then, more weary than he knew, he shrugged. "Suit yourself."

Ross tossed and turned restlessly. Every fiber of his body cried out for sleep, but no matter how he courted it, sleep would not come. The harder he tried to relax, the less he succeeded. Frustrated and irritable, with his hands pillowing his head, as if it were her fault, he glared at Antonia through slitted lids.

For what seemed an eternity she sat without moving. A graven image cast into shadow by the dying fire. Then with the grace of a flower swaying in the wind, she took up her brush and began to brush her hair. Slowly, the rhythm mesmerizing, she tried to work through the tangle. Ross didn't know from what part of his lost memory the knowledge came, but watching her, he knew why he couldn't sleep.

He didn't like admitting the need, or that his arms ached from more than weariness, but no matter how he tried, the need was still there. And the ache. "Hell!" he muttered and flung aside the covers. With his head protesting the sudden move, he went to her, taking the brush from her hand. Ignoring her gasp of surprise he knelt at her side and concentrated on working free the tangle.

"Ouch!" Antonia's head jerked as he tugged the brush through her hair.

"Sorry." He didn't sound sorry, but his touch grew gentler, the strokes of the brush longer, more deliberate. Patience accomplished what busywork hadn't and frustration couldn't. When the tangle was free and her hair flowed smoothly down her back, he tossed the brush aside. "Done."

"Thanks."

"I don't need thanks. I need sleep." Rising, he offered his hand. "Come to bed."

When she finally looked up at him the expression on her face was one he couldn't read. Her eyes were dark and fathomless. A look of fear? Surely she wasn't afraid of him! Ross's frustration turned to unreasoning anger. "Dammit, woman!" He exploded. "I'm not going to attack you."

Pain ricocheted through his head nearly driving him to his knees. "Hell," he groaned softly, "I couldn't if I wanted to." He passed unsteady fingers over his eyes, staggering as he did.

"I never thought..." Antonia stopped, aware that locked in his pain, he didn't hear her. He remembered nothing of the days and nights of delirium when he fought himself and her. Sweating and cursing, until she discovered he quieted when she held him and slept in his arms.

Habit or subconscious need? It didn't matter.

"Please." His hands dropped to his side as if he hadn't the strength for more.

She was already rising to him. His face was ghastly as she slipped her arm around him and led him to their bed.

"Maybe." He drew her down to him, holding her tightly. "Maybe we'd better wait another day to go down the mountain."

"Maybe," Antonia agreed, but he was already asleep.

Five

―――――

"You're kidding!" With the dull, colorless sun of morning at her back, Antonia watched his haggard face for some sign that this was a joke. Humor under stress. A smile for survival.

Hands on his hips, Ross returned her look soberly.

"Okay." She grimaced. "So, you're not kidding."

"I'm not kidding. I'm not playing at being gallant. And this isn't the Me, Tarzan, You, Jane Hour, either." Ross didn't look at the source of her objections, backpacks he'd fashioned out of parts scavenged from the wreckage. First by Antonia, then himself.

"I'm supposed to believe it's fair that I'm carrying this little bag?" She gestured in disgust at the markedly smaller of the two packs, then at the larger. "While you carry that?"

"Antonia . . ."

"First you think I'm an airhead with tinsel for brains. Now, for some inscrutable reason, because of these—" she waved again at the packs "—you're worried about my big toe?" She shook her head and rolled her eyes heavenward.

"He's worried about my big toe! Men have concerned themselves with certain parts of my body, but my big toe?"

"Antonia, listen—"

"Ross, let's wait." Worry replaced irony in her voice as she looked at the violent discolorations that marked his forehead and cheek. "Just for another day or two, until you're thinking clearer. Before the crash you said I should stay with the plane. Then why shouldn't we both? Dare might..."

"Dammit, Antonia!" He flung up an arm, wanting to twine his hands in her loose, flowing hair and shake her, making her see what he saw, and understand, as he did, the coming danger. Yet he knew it wasn't that she was being foolish, or obtuse. His gaze swept over her, seeing the intelligence in those wide gray eyes that stared in surprise. She was only untutored in the way of the land. Now it had fallen to him to teach her the formidable, with none of the good. That, not Antonia's innocence, was the rationale for his anger.

Folding his splayed fingers into his palm, he dropped his arm to his side. His voice was quieter, even gentle. "Dare isn't coming, at least not in time."

"In time!" Antonia's face paled. "What is it? What's wrong?" Her fingers clutched the leather of his jacket sleeve. "Your condition's worsened!"

"No." His sudden fit of temper ebbed. Her fear was for him, not herself. It hadn't taken sleeping in a bed of silks and furs, twined in her soothing arms for Ross to discover that beneath the glamour lay a tender heart. He'd seen it with Jacinda, with Tyler and the twins. Nevertheless he hadn't let himself believe.

"Leave the wood." He glanced down at the fallen limbs and sticks she'd gathered. A chore she'd taken upon herself from the first. "We have more than enough for now. Come with me away from the cold."

At her quiet agreement, he walked with her to their shelter where a small camp fire burned. Taking her hands he drew her down to the scattered bits of clothing that looked more like the mayhem of a bacchanalian tryst than the bed of virtue and comfort it had been. Kneeling before her as she sat cross-legged amid the rainbow of apparel, he kept her hands in his. "I hoped it wouldn't come to this. Not yet. Now it has. We have to leave here. Today. Within the hour in fact, but it has nothing to do with my condition."

"Within the hour?" She gripped his hands remembering, in spite of his protests, the restlessness, the incoherence, the sickness that once left him weak and trembling. Though he hadn't admitted more than a dull ache behind his eyes in the past twenty-four hours and his touch was steady, his face showed the ravages of illness. He was tired. So tired. Yet in designing the packs he'd demonstrated ingenuity and clarity of thought.

That, per chance, was most telling of all.

Antonia wanted desperately to believe in her judgment, to believe him. "Then tell me why. Why must we leave here?" she asked softly. "The truth. All of it."

"The truth in a word, weather."

"Weather?" Antonia was surprised at the terseness of his answer, the tight worried cast of his expression.

In the storm that followed the crash, thunder had shaken the ground as fiercely as an earthquake. Great, jagged bolts of lightning virtually exploded a grove of trees at the clearing's edge. Splintered limbs had flown like burning brands in all directions, mercifully, none on ground soaked by fuel. Nature had done its worst. Yet nothing, not thunder, not lightning, nor blowing rain had touched them while they drowsed and slept, emotionally and physically exhausted but secure in their stone-lined lair.

If they could withstand the fury of the first thunderstorm of spring, surely Ross wouldn't be so worried over another. "It's more than just a storm, isn't it?"

Ross didn't look at her, instead he glanced at the high, thin cirrus clouds filled with ice and snow. Their dingy gray had faded to white, and drifts that looked like white mares' tails were rising, reaching new heights.

Heavy weather in twenty-four hours. The unmistakable signs were there. A ring around the moon the night before. The morning's red dawn. The ominous stillness of the air.

He explained them all to her, carefully, in any detail she wished. "Snow, Antonia. Everything points to it." He completed his instruction with the latest warnings. "The smell in the air, the temperature, sun dogs, and intuition."

"Sun dogs?" Antonia barely remembered seeing the sun, and the term was foreign to her.

"A halo around the sun, an ancient omen of rain or snow." Ross answered her implied question. "Don't ask where the name originated, I haven't any idea."

"But it's spring."

"It's March, a maverick month with the best and the worst and our most volatile weather. The more dangerous snowstorms can come in March. At this altitude, it could be a killer. We have to get down. Even a thousand feet could make a difference."

A thousand feet didn't sound like much, but as she remembered the rugged mountains that bordered this small, sharp peak, she knew it could be an impossible distance. Her grip on his hands tightened convulsively. "How long?"

"A day, if we're lucky."

She searched his face in the gloom cast by the rock ledge. Gloom that deepened as the morning had gone on. Drawing one hand from his she curved her palm around the dark evidence of his injury. "Are you sure?"

"That I can make it? I can. I've grown stronger every hour. The extra days of rest helped. You were right in that, but now the choice has been taken out of our hands. Whether I could make it or not, we would have to go down the mountain."

Antonia nodded, her hand slid from his face and she looked away, waiting for his instructions.

Ross felt the heat of her touch, as if her hand hadn't left him. His gaze went to her temple, marked by the cut that skirted the hairline. It defied reason that a woman whose looks were an integral part of her profession should be so little concerned with herself. Concussion could be potentially dangerous and a scary experience for the uninitiated. His bruised brain would heal leaving him unmarked. Her torn flesh would heal. He had done his best with the little he had to work with, within the time element, to see that she would.

But there was nothing he could do that would keep her from scarring.

He knew the scar disturbed her. It wouldn't be human not to regret the marring of such beautiful skin. Yet she refused to dwell on it, accepting what nothing could change with astonishing poise. Ross closed his eyes, he saw the cut, red and angry, as it had been this morning when he cleansed it. As he had every morning since his mind had been his own and his thoughts unclouded.

She was a quick healer, and there would be no infection. But what he'd done was too little, far too late.

Ross drew back from his anger at the fate that had done this to her. Back from the anger with himself, at his failure to protect her. In the end, he knew Antonia's conviction was wisest. Railing at himself and providence was a waste of precious energy. The past was ended. Only the future was crucial.

The future. When he thought of it, of the task ahead of a bewitching tenderfoot and a newly unbefuddled yokel, he wondered if they faced the impossible.

"Patrick did it." His words, though low and hoarse, were like the crack of a rifle in the hovering quiet. At Antonia's sharply drawn breath, he realized that his thoughts had wandered. "Sorry, I was thinking out loud, not hallucinating. I'd almost forgotten. Patrick McCallum's corporate plane went down in the mountains years ago with Rafe Courtenay, the CEO, and Patrick onboard. The pilot was killed, Rafe sustained a severe head injury and was semi-paralyzed. Patrick's leg was shattered, yet he walked out and brought Rafe with him."

Sliding his fingers around hers he raised their locked hands before them, keeping palm to palm, wrist to wrist, in a gladiator's salute. "If Patrick can do it alone, we can do it together." He grinned a wicked, challenging grin. "Are you game, sweetheart?"

Even the shadows could not darken the fierce glow of his brilliant blue eyes. She couldn't avoid the probing look that seemed to reach into her searching for more than an answer to his challenge.

Searching for trust.

Antonia realized that she did trust him. That she had since a silly little truce, made and broken, then made again. This time she knew it wouldn't be broken.

Her fingers tightened, returning the pressure of his clasp. She would trust him, and follow wherever he led. Beyond their hands, their gazes held, steady gray and cool blue. A gauntlet thrown by one, taken up by two.

Softly, her lips barely moving, she murmured, "Game." Then almost as an afterthought she added, "Doc."

He grinned, a slow, devilish grin and released her hand. For a heated instant Antonia thought he meant to pat her on the head saying something typical like what a brave, little movie star she was, or another patronizing little cliché. Before the flash of indignation materialized, with his eyes still holding hers, his wicked grin softened into something that made her mouth go dry instead. In that exquisite eternity, she discovered she wanted him to touch her again.

With color rising in her cheeks and a misbehaving heart, she rushed to hide her discomfort. "I'll follow you, Doc," she drawled lazily, bringing a lighter mood to the electric moment. "But before I go even one step I intend to know what my big toe has to do with anything."

"Right." Ross laughed and ruffled her hair. Climbing to his knees, then his feet, he stood over her. "I'll make a pot of tea. It may be our last for a while. As we drink it, we'll go over plans for the journey down. And," he said, chuckling as he turned away, "the importance of your toe."

Half an hour later, her mind was slightly dazed from all Ross had explained, but she understood the finer points of walking. Specifically walking in the wilderness. They would be traveling untamed country, over steep and rugged terrain. Ross had resolved the mystery of the digit in question by explaining that walking employed more than a hundred different muscles, but the propulsive thrust began with the big toe.

Antonia nodded that she understood. She even agreed with the premise that one must keep a sensible and even distribution of weight while walking in order to keep the propulsion painless. Then he lost her in a digression into the difficulties of physical and chemical differences between men and women as they related to walking. When he ventured further, into overexertion, lactic acid in the blood and poor muscle performance that required hours for recovery, she surrendered.

"I give up." She set her second cup of tea aside. "I'll carry the smaller pack."

"I thought you might," Ross observed innocently. Too innocently.

"Might what? Give up on your discourse or accept the smaller pack?"

"Both." Ross smiled and continued examining supplies he'd assembled for their trek. The disparate heap seemed to spring from the dust at his feet. Most intriguing were the packs constructed of metal bars and a rectangular tarp taken from the nether regions of the plane. The rough cloth had been cut, folded and lashed to the makeshift frame. The provisions that would go in them were meager. They would be traveling light, as much out of necessity as lack of supplies.

"You have everything under control, so what sense is there in fighting?" Why fight, indeed? Watching him, listening to him, she'd realized how competent he was. No, he was more than competent. Far more. Ross was a master woodsman. If there was luck in any of this it was that in facing the dangers of this wild land, it was Ross who held her life in his skilled hands.

Subconsciously she brushed her hair from her temple, remembering when his hands had been gentle as well.

"Not everything, Antonia."

"Pardon?" She hadn't realized that he'd finished his packing and risen to his feet.

"I said," he spoke deliberately, every word clearly enunciated, "not everything is under control."

Antonia looked blankly from Ross to the waiting packs, and back again. He had moved so purposefully, what could be left to do?

"You, Antonia," he said, looking down at her as she huddled on the flat plane of a granite slab. "You aren't ready. Your clothing to be exact. And your hair." He leaned to gather into one hand the dark strands that tumbled down her back. "There are briers out there. They'll claw and tug at you, and draw blood when they can. Worst of all they'll snag this beautiful stuff, trapping you and holding you as surely as any shackle.

"First we'll see what your wardrobe offers, then I'll braid your hair."

"I can braid it."

"I never for a minute thought you couldn't." Ignoring the confounded look on her face he turned to her luggage and began pawing through it. A major portion of her clothing had contributed to their bed, but only the softly delicate pieces. Pieces unsuited for his purpose now.

As he tossed one article of clothing after another from her bag, Antonia said with as much restraint as she could, "If you would tell me what you're looking for, I might find it quicker."

"Something loose but warm." He drew out an iridescent unitard in spandex. Holding it between two fingers as if it were something obnoxious, he discarded it muttering, "Something that breathes and won't drown you in sweat onc minute then freeze you in it the next." Sitting back on his haunches he watched her watch him. "You do sweat, don't you? If you haven't, sweetheart, you will. Believe me, you will."

Before Antonia could form a reply he was tumbling the remaining clothing from the case.

"Is this what you're looking for?" Snatching up a pair of faded jeans she let them dangle from her fingers.

"Well, well. Will wonders never cease. Why didn't you tell me you had these?"

"If I'd known you were looking for them I would have."

Ross grinned at her and gestured at the small mountain of clothing. "I don't suppose you have a loose cotton sweater or sweatshirt in here."

"As a matter of fact..." One deft move produced a beautiful creation, a multicolored collage in knitted cotton. Another move brought out a red sweatshirt so old it had faded to deep rose.

Ross caught up the faded jeans pairing them with the faded shirt. "Disgraceful." He clicked his tongue in mock despair. "Tell me how a genteel lady like you came to have such a marvelously disreputable outfit?"

"Genteel ladies, as you so sweetly call them, have their ungenteel moments. If they didn't, they'd choke on their boas."

"Would they now? What do you do when you wear these?" He asked casually, yet it was anything but a casual question. Ross wondered why he cared, except he figured she would be damnably lovely, flushed and tousled, dressed in old jeans and a faded sweatshirt. Lovely and real.

"I keep a horse. When the pressure gets to me, I ride."

"In these?" He lifted incredulous eyes to hers. "What, no pink jacket, and English saddle?"

"Western." Antonia's answer was a little short. "And these." Taking the clothing from him she added, "When I said *keep* a horse, I meant exactly that. I comb Solita. I curry her. I clean her stable. When I'm away, someone else assumes those duties, but when I ride, they're mine. An old habit left over from childhood."

"I take it you didn't cut your teeth on boas?"

"Boas were hard to come by in small southern towns."

"But you learned to ride there?"

"My mom couldn't abide dogs, but she didn't mind horses."

"A black horse?"

Antonia laughed. "Black as sin. How did you guess?"

"Wishful thinking, maybe." He missed the perplexed look she shot him. He was too preoccupied with the image of Antonia racing the black horse, her black hair flying. The old shirt would have been new then, a splash of scarlet against the glossy mane as she bent low over the horse's neck.

Magnificent. God! She would have been utterly magnificent.

"There's a wool sweater here somewhere."

"Wool?" Ross concentrated as the vision faded.

"For cold mornings. Sometimes on location, if a horse can be found, I ride at dawn. My riding habit, you might call it, goes with me everywhere."

"A lucky thing for us this time." Good, Ross thought, it was doubtful she realized it, but she understood already the basic principle of heat loss. "We'll begin with this next to your skin." He handed her a finely woven cotton shirt. "And then this."

This, was a second shirt of washed silk, heavier than the first, more tightly woven. Antonia took it, and the next, and the next, until her arms were filled.

"Put them on in order." He was retrieving discarded clothing, stuffing it back into her bag. "If one is too tight, pitch it and choose another. Each layer of clothing must be looser than the one before it. What you wear will depend on the weather. The wool if it's bitter cold. When you're warm, the layers you're wearing can be peeled away one at a time. If it rains, this." He held up the cotton sweater, praying rain was the worst they would have to contend with.

His gaze probed her body. Not even the jacket she wore, silk again, could hide her ample breasts. Breasts that had pillowed his head as he struggled with the madness and shock of concussion. "I assume you, more than most, understand the importance of support. Be sure your lingerie is comfortable, that nothing chafes, especially at your shoulders where the pack straps will rest.

"There's no help for your shoes. Most are too fragile for the terrain we'll be covering. Your boots are sturdy, but too stiff. The leather sneakers will have to serve." He frowned, damning himself that he'd been distracted by Jacinda's early-morning call and her absurd plan that he and Antonia should travel together. Too distracted to see to proper emergency supplies for her. Particularly proper footwear. There was no help for his dereliction now.

"Change." The word was an order, barked with the edge of ever-threatening anger. The anger was in part the natural mood swings and irritability that followed brain injuries, in part frustration and McLachlan temper. He knew and understood that it was directed at himself, but Antonia didn't. Her silence was a testament to that.

"Look, none of this is your fault." He forced a congeniality into his words that neither their situation nor his conditions merited. And from the startled look on her face, his clumsy attempt to rectify his anger only succeeded in disturbing her more. "Oh, hell!" He spun on his heel and left her, tossing final instructions over his shoulder. "Just get dressed."

Antonia watched him go. She was not smarting or stunned by his ill temper. After all, she'd spent a week coping with his vacillations. She knew he fought now against those erratic mood swings. That he was a physician and recognized them for what they were, didn't make them any less bewildering. The stress of enforced idleness as he regained his strength, coupled now with apprehension of the ordeal ahead magnified every emotion. He was like an unpredictable bear cub. Playful one minute, snarling out his frustrations the next.

"So that's how it's to be," she muttered as she scooped up the clothing he'd practically flung at her. She wasn't exactly the least temperamental creature to come down the pike, either, but at least she could empathize with his distress and deal with it. Unconsciously she fell into a habit left over from a childhood spent virtually alone. Lecturing herself in a singsong half whisper she began to change.

"Don't bite when he barks, Antonia." Given their history she wouldn't deceive herself that it would be easy. Absently she began to fumble with buttons and zippers.

"Tolerance." Nothing to it. She'd been tolerant all her life. Slipping out of her jacket she tossed her blouse aside with it.

"Compassion." Yeah. She could do that one. It was like tolerance. Easy. What hardly resembled her once highly polished boots slipped from her feet.

"Patience." Uh-oh. That one might take a little practice. But maybe, if she didn't backslide too often...? Suede slacks slid down long, slender legs and were kicked away.

"Love."

That one brought her up short.

"Now where did that come from?" She frowned, then she laughed.

"Habit." With a shake of her head she shrugged it away. When one was born and had grown to adolescence in the Bible Belt of the south, love followed tolerance, compassion and patience as naturally as John followed Matthew, Mark, Luke and...

Antonia laughed again and flung her hair back from her face.

Clad only in a lacy camisole and clinging tap pants she leaned to the dancing light of the fire, letting its warmth drift over her skin before she began to dress. Caught up in her sybaritic ritual she didn't notice Ross standing just beyond the shelter, his hand braced against a jutting rock, his call lying unspoken on his tongue.

It wasn't Antonia nor the half-whispered incantation that stopped him in his tracks. It was her laughter. The low, winsome sound of it wound around him like a caress as her lovely, shapely shadow danced over stone walls, holding him spellbound. As the day had grown somber beneath a cover of clouds, the fire had grown brighter. In the still air it leaped and swayed as if it were a mischievous child, painting masterpieces on canvases of granite just for him.

With his mouth dry, and his breath drawn deeply, Ross watched as the shadow dancer, *his* dancer, lifted her arms and, by a trick of the light, the simple act of dressing became a pagan rite. Elegant, erotic, primal. An exquisite woman, a graceful willow, a rainbow in misty shades of ebony painted by fire...his shadow dancer was all of them. But none was as magnificent as the original.

He didn't turn to her, he didn't dare. Different lives, different worlds and four years of antagonism stood between them. The wilderness could temper it and even make them forget, but it wouldn't change it.

Nothing would change it. No one could.

The boulder was hot from his touch, his eyes burned, his lungs ached for air. Carefully, her image still etched in his mind, he backed away. One step, and then another, until the alcove was in darkness and no shadow danced.

Even in its calm the air was biting, the breath he hungered for was frigid. The temperature had plummeted. Lowering clouds barely hung in the sky, their hidden depth swollen and seething with the imminent birth of the storm.

They had to move. Now.

"Ross."

Until her voice, until her touch, he hadn't realized that he stood with arms taut and hands fisted, glaring at the sky. Slowly, half expecting to see the shadowy enchantress, he looked down at her. "Antonia." His voice was husky with memory.

"Ready?"

He looked down at her hand on his sleeve, then at Antonia. She was dressed as he'd asked. The jeans were snug without being too tight at thigh and knee. Shirts and blouses of many hues peeked from the collar of the once-scarlet sweatshirt. Her hair tumbled unbound down her back. Ross remembered that he had wanted to braid it. "Yes, I'm ready."

Choosing a seat he pulled her back against him, fitting her between his thighs. Then, as if the storm did not threaten, as if there were all the time in the world, he wove her hair into one heavy braid. When he was done, he tucked it beneath her shirt. Then with careful fingers he examined the cut at her temple. His satisfied nod was for her phenomenal healing, not for the scar he couldn't block from his mind. When there was nothing left to do, he sat, hands on her shoulders, letting her fragrance mingle with the cold in his lungs.

Antonia laid a hand on his where it rested on her shoulder. She couldn't see his face, but sensed the strangeness of his mood. Keeping her own counsel, abiding by her newly determined tolerance, she said simply, "Thank you."

"My pleasure," Ross replied and discovered that he meant it. Here in a world where every move was accompanied by raw desperation, he'd found a quiet diversion in the feel of her hair sliding through his fingers as the scent of moss and wild roses soothed a savage, unnamed need.

He knew he should move, setting into motion the last check. The trail down would not be made easier by delay. The storm would not wait. But he was oddly reluctant to relinquish this small contentment.

He drew a long, deep breath and thought of a summer's night, of moonlight and dewy roses.

Antonia lifted her face toward the sky. It was still early morning, but the cloud cover had turned it as dim as twilight. She sensed the changes Ross had, the arctic cold, the alarming hush, the sinister sky, and felt the same reluctance.

His hand slid down her arm to her hand. His palm pressed against hers, his fingers gripped tightly. A gentle reminder for both of them of a challenge made by one, accepted by two. With only the barest nod of her head, Antonia sighed and rose from his embrace. Hands still clasped they walked together to the shelter.

Then it was Ross's time to nod his approval. The fire had been drowned, then covered with dirt. Clothing they would be leaving behind had been collected and stuffed into luggage. Only the packs lay waiting for them.

"Frightened?" he murmured.

"Out of my wits."

"So am I," he admitted. "Only a fool wouldn't be."

When Antonia bent to pick up her pack, he was there before her. "I can do this."

"I never said you couldn't," he said as he had before, and as before, it was he who completed the chore. When he stepped back the pack was fitted comfortably and securely over her shoulders. Shrugging into his own, he adjusted it just as carefully. The comfort of the pack, as with the fit of the shoes, could become critical.

Leading the way through the debris, he paused at the edge of the clearing. While she had cleaned the shelter, he had been busy himself. Sheets of torn metal turned with the unpainted side to the sun to serve as reflectors had been lifted onto taller boulders. The coming snow would bury them, but not so deeply now as it would have on the ground. When it melted, it would melt first on the stone, and would stand starkly apart from the snow. One heap of scrap had been formed into an arrow, pointing the way they would be going.

"If Dare finds it, he'll know," Antonia said in an undertone as she realized what he'd done.

"*When* Dare finds it, he'll know."

"When," Antonia corrected herself with a suddenly wobbly smile.

"Who knows, sweetheart, we may be down the mountain and home before he can even search this sector."

"But not if we stand here for much longer."

"The lady has a point." He grinned and tugged at the braid tucked snugly away from harm. His smile faded, the pad of his thumb stroked the line of her jaw to her chin. "Follow closely. Step as nearly as you can in my tracks. The underbrush is dense and the going will be rough. If we're lucky we might find a game track going our way. If you're ever uncomfortable, don't be reluctant to tell me. If you need to rest, don't push it.

"This isn't a contest of stamina. Nobody says you should be as ugly or as strong as I am, or that I have to be as pretty and brave as you are. The keyword is together. We're pooling our strengths to cancel out our weaknesses, but it won't work unless we're as honest about one as the other.

"One more thing." From his pocket he took two knitted caps. One he fitted over her head, the other on his own. Both were tugged low over forehead and ears. Ross grimaced and mugged and Antonia laughed as he intended she should.

"Who did you say was pretty?" She tugged at her cap until only her gray eyes glittered above a bright pink nose.

"You are. Anywhere. Anytime."

"Ha! You didn't think so a week ago."

"Didn't I?" Ross's thumb moved from her chin to her lower lip, tracing its line, slowly, gently, watching as her smile faltered. "What did a country yokel know about movie stars a week ago?"

"As much and as little as I knew of you." His fingers were warm against her skin in the bite of the cold.

"That makes us even, doesn't it?"

Antonia nodded, not sure she trusted her voice when he looked at her as he did now.

"We can do this, Antonia." Ross's voice was low, but strong. "Together."

"Yes, together."

Ross stared hard at her, then he nodded. When he turned to begin the trek down the mountain, he didn't need to look back to know that Antonia followed.

Six

Antonia stopped and with a forearm wiped the sweat from her eyes. Ross had promised that she would sweat, and even though it was bitterly cold, that's exactly what she'd done. Sweat.

The result of exertion, of fighting her way through thickets and patches of briers that closed around her like a living prison. Even as Ross blazed a trail for her with his body and his steady pace, every step was a battle that beaded her brow with a sheen of moisture. All the heat came from inside her, from the center of her chest, fooling the rest of her body into thinking she wasn't cold.

Until she stopped.

A mistake, stopping. Her breath was a white mist as she sighed and its fleeting warmth teased her nose. Her eyes were dry and grainy and burned. Freeze-dried? she wondered. A hoarse chuckle rumbled beneath layers and layers of clothing. At least she could still laugh.

With her hands on her hips she stretched, and discovered nerves and sinews she'd forgotten existed. Ross declared that walking utilized approximately a hundred muscles. When they stopped for . . . she realized she didn't remember which stop was next. Was it lunch? Or had they already done that? Dinner? Or just one of the frequent rest stops he insisted on? Was it of any consequence? For among her many discomforts, hunger wasn't one of them. She'd nibbled constantly on the trail at Ross's insistence. Nuts, raisins, dates, even a bit of hard cheese. They'd eaten and walked. Always downward, always through brutal underbrush, for so many hours her mind was numb and with her watch damaged in the crash she'd completely lost track of time.

The gray day was no help. It had simply gotten grayer. Grayer and darker. Under the dense canopy of trees time lost its meaning. Was it dusk, or twilight, or was evening approaching? Antonia discovered she didn't care. But when they stopped, she would tell Ross he should count again. Walking took far more than a hundred muscles, and now she knew each of them intimately.

Her neck ached, her shoulders ached, the small of her back and her ribs. Her thighs ached, her calves ached. Her feet, bless them, were too numb to ache, but she was sure they did. Her knees had gone beyond aching. They were million-year-old hinges that had to be broken free of rust with each step.

At first as they'd walked, Ross had talked and pointed out what he felt she should know. Then as the hours crept by and the cold had crept in, her mind became an automaton concerned only with the desperate act of putting one foot in front of the other, and he had grown silent.

They'd gone down, always down with no ease in terrain, no trails to aid them. And now she couldn't take another step. Not for Ross, or herself, not for anyone ever again.

"Antonia?"

She could have sworn she'd only dawdled for a second, but Ross had stopped two hundred feet down the trail. In the distance, with the waxy green leaves of mountain laurel crowding around him in the murky light, she could see the worry on his face. Complaints she'd been determined to voice died on her lips. He was as tired as she. As cold. If his muscles didn't ache as much, his head must shriek in agony.

"Just taking a breather," she called to him.

The wild shrub that brushed his shoulder was clustered under a towering evergreen. The same tree painted on the tail of the plane they'd left. She hoped that it was its shadow that turned his face gray, but knew it was the cold, the strain, worry for her.

"There's a small cul-de-sac down the trail. I caught a glimpse of it a while ago from the edge of the ravine we skirted. It would offer natural shelter for the night if you can go a little farther." When she didn't answer, he reached for the straps of his pack. "Or we can stop here, if you'd like."

"No!" She shifted her own pack to a more comfortable position. "Let's go on. I can make it."

"A few more feet one way or the other won't matter."

"They matter," Antonia disagreed and so, truly, did he. "Every bit we travel down this mountain matters."

"Antonia." He took a step back toward her.

"No!" She stopped him with an upraised hand. Any progress was too precious to negate by moving back even an inch.

"Antonia, you're exhausted."

"I can make it." She put one foot in front of the other, and then another. Her rusted knees protested with each effort, but she kept her face blank. "I can make it," she said as her foot went down again. Her teeth were clenched, the muscles in her throat were straining. "I *will* make it."

It hurt to see her so tired. Ross wanted to go to her, to tell her she needn't try so hard. But he knew that she must. Today and the days after. She had to try, and he knew she wouldn't thank him for his sympathy.

It would be his responsibility to shepherd her stamina. But she must never know.

The cul-de-sac was only a small distance away. He had set her a goal. One she could meet without drastic inroads into her resilience. A sense of accomplishment would blunt the agony of fatigue. He watched her carefully as she moved with renewed determination. Thank God, he hadn't misjudged her reserve.

"Not much farther." He offered what little encouragement he dared.

"Right."

She didn't look up. He didn't expect she would. All her energies, all her thoughts were focused on the next step.

"Five more minutes and you can rest."

"Rest?" Her lips barely moved. "What's that and who needs it?"

"Who?" he asked, so proud of her his heart was nearly bursting. "I do, sweetheart. I do."

He turned away to begin his own descent. He did see her smile, however grim, but still a smile, as she recognized his efforts for what they were.

"I can do this," she muttered. "I can. I won't hold him back." But she was already holding him back. Ross was an experienced woodsman, and even with the aftereffects of his concussion he could have moved faster and covered greater distances without her. She might be an albatross around his neck, but, she vowed as she took the next step and the next, she wouldn't drown him.

Ross was the woodsman. His world was real. She was the actress. Hers was an imaginary world, a world of pretending. So, she would make what she knew work for her. She would pretend.

"Moss grows thickest on the shadiest side of the tree." Her voice was low, but steady. This wasn't the woods, and she wasn't cold, and her knees felt wonderful. The lines she was reciting were from an exciting new screenplay, excerpts from "Ross McLachlan's Discourse for a Ramble in the Woods."

Not exactly a catchy title, and there would be trouble fitting it on a marquee, but it would do, until something better came along.

"The shadiest side, where the moss grows, will be North. A good rule of thumb to remember, my dear, except—" she wagged a cautioning finger without noticing she did "—except, one must *also* remember that certain mosses like the sun." A humorless chuckle rumbled in her throat. "Then what the hell do you, oh fellow woodsman?"

Without missing a beat she launched into the next little tidbit meant to help one stay alive in the woods. "Tops of pines and hemlocks point toward the rising sun, which of course, is east. *Unless* the winds turn them in another direction.

"Well, I'll be switched!" The colloquialism from her childhood tumbled out as naturally as if she were still eight and sat in her grandmother's kitchen. But it was Antonia the star, not the child who drawled, "And here I thought hemlock was for poisoning people."

Skirting an uncommonly vicious copse of thorns, she extracted herself from one particularly persistent little devil with distracted ease and continued her dissertation. "Trees fall in the direction of the prevailing wind, *so long* as there have been no deviations. Ah-ha! If one was there to know, then one was there before. So, *one* isn't lost, is she?"

Her foot slipped on a slick rock and she went down hard. The weight of her pack tipped her backward taking the brunt of the impact. Yet, even its cushioning wasn't enough to keep her from clamping her teeth on her lip with such force that it drew blood. As soon as she could catch her breath again, she scrambled up. A quick glance down the trail told her that her descent into ignominy hadn't been observed. Ross's view of her was temporarily obscured by the underbrush. He mustn't know. He had too much to contend with to be troubled by her gracelessness.

With a swipe at her lip, and a hitch for her pack, she began again. One foot following the other, this time with more care. She coughed and a sharp pain caught her in its vise. Stifling a groan she forced herself to breath, shallowly at first, then deeper, until her chest hurt only a little more than the rest of her.

"Now," she muttered when the worst had passed, "where was I? The woods, silly, how could you forget?" She was back to the self-hypnotizing dissertation.

"Growth rings. What about growth rings?" For a moment she drew a blank. Another rock, looking slicker that the last, loomed before her. Giving it a wide berth she searched her memory. "Ah, yes! Growth rings of a tree are wider toward the sun. That way... another of course here—" a sotto voce observation intended for no one but herself, "—is east. And so, *on*, my fellow woodsman,

woodswoman, woods*person*, what do you do if you don't
have an ax?''

She collided with Ross. Only his arms closing around her
kept her from falling. When she looked up, he was laughing.

"Jacinda said you speak in italics, but I didn't believe
her." He could hardly believe as well, that she could recite,
nearly verbatim, all he'd told her on the trail. She'd given it
her own personal twist, but she remembered. Antonia Russell was a quick study. The brains in that lovely head weren't
tinsel.

"An old habit, one I thought I'd broken." His arms felt
so good, his body was such solid support that even as tired
as she was, she didn't want to move to sit or lie down. Quite
without realizing what she did, she laid her head on his chest
and closed her eyes. Layer upon layer of clothing separated
them but did not disguise the hard musculature of his lean
frame. For the first time since they'd left the clearing, she
felt secure. She wanted to sink into him and never move
again.

He tugged the knitted cap from her head. "You aren't
falling asleep on me are you?"

"I was considering it."

"How about a cup of hot chocolate before you do?"

For the first time she saw he had a fire going with a kettle
of water set to boil. Had he made quick work of it or had
she fallen that far behind? She didn't care. She was here
now, and when he held her she was almost warm.

"Antonia, did you hear me?"

"I thought I might be dreaming. Did you say hot chocolate?"

"You aren't dreaming. It's Dare's specialty. A mix he
makes up by the buckets. I found a container today, under
what was your seat in the plane. It would be better with milk
but, in a pinch, water will do."

Now that she'd stopped, Antonia wasn't sure she could
walk another step, not even to the shelter of stones, or the
warmth of the fire. Seeming to read her mind, Ross eased
the pack's straps from her shoulders and slid it to the
ground. Before she knew what he meant to do, he lifted her

into his arms. He was exhausted, he was hurt, yet he carried her to the fireside as if she were weightless.

"I should help," she protested as he lowered her to a bed of leaves he'd covered with a shirt.

He crouched at her side, tucking a silky wisp of black behind her ear. "There's nothing for you to do but rest."

"But—"

"Shh." His hand covered her lips. "You talk too much." He laughed as a flash of anger turned her eyes the color of smoke. "I reckoned that one would get to you. And you thought you were too frazzled to ever feel anything again." Grinning, he watched her expressive eyes change again as she guessed what he was doing. "If I take my hand away, will you stop arguing?"

Antonia nodded slowly, and Ross watched her eyes change once more. He'd seen anger, surprise and laughter, all exquisitely conveyed in shades of gray by her marvelous eyes. Eyes a man could lose himself in.

"Promise." He was surprised by the roughness in his voice. Clearing his throat, he began again. "Promise."

Another nod, and now her eyes were solemn.

God help him. He was going to drown in them. His teeth were clenched, but his face was blank as he lifted his hand from her mouth. "Hot chocolate coming . . . hey!" He interrupted himself. Cupping her chin in his palm he turned her face toward the firelight. "What's this?"

"It's nothing." Antonia tried to turn her head away.

He muttered a fierce oath and held her even tighter, his gaze riveted on the small curved cut across her lower lip. "What happened? And don't tell me nothing did. Don't even try."

"Okay." She gestured abruptly, her vow of patience forgotten. "I fell. Like a clumsy idiot, I sprawled over the forest floor."

"Where? When? Why didn't you tell me?" He drew a deep, ragged breath. "Dammit, Antonia, are you hurt?"

"If you keep saying that I'm going to start thinking it's my first name. Dammit Antonia Russell. That should look very nice on a marquee." Right under "Ross McLachlan's Discourse for a Ramble in the Woods."

"Tell me!" His hands were at her shoulders now, gripping too hard. Then, unexpectedly his hold loosened. He didn't release her but his touch was gentle. "Are you hurt?"

He hadn't heard a word of her satire. Not one. Antonia recalled his caution that even a minor problem could become life threatening in the wild. It was that concern he was reacting to.

"I'm not hurt." She covered his hand with her own. "I slipped on a rock. The pack took the major force of the impact, so all that suffered was my pride, and this." Brushing a fingertip over the cut, she smiled. "I've had worse when my lips were chapped."

His eyes narrowed as if he didn't quite believe her. Then he nodded. "Yeah, I suppose you have."

Moving away, he crouched over the fire, adding wood to the small blaze. His back was to her as he reached into his pack and drew out a plastic container. With a practiced hand he measured a mixture of chocolate, sugar and powdered milk into two cups. The battered aluminum kettle had begun to steam. Using a spare shirt to wrap the handle, he filled the cups. Almost instantly the tiny space of their new camp was redolent with the fragrance of rich, dark chocolate. And incredibly, of cinnamon.

Antonia closed her eyes, wondering if anything had ever smelled so good.

"My apologies, Sleeping Beauty." He knelt over her again, handing her a cup. "No marshmallows."

"I'll try to muddle through."

"Could you eat some stew?" He was speaking of the packaged, freeze-dried foods he kept as a matter of course in the plane, rescued after the crash by Antonia.

"Stew?" That would mean he'd found water to replenish their depleted supply from the seep on the mountain-top.

With a gesture to their left he said, "There's a stream just beyond that rise. We'll follow it down tomorrow. If we're lucky, it will lead us to some sort of settlement."

Antonia knew she should be excited about the stream, about the prospect of a settlement, but she was too tired for excitement. Too tired to eat.

"This is enough for me." She lifted the cup and sipped the cinnamon-flavored chocolate. Then, folding her hands around the heated plastic she leaned back against a moss-covered rock. As she drank the reviving liquid, she really looked at her surroundings for the first time.

Ross's choice for their camp was a circle of boulders. This time none was taller than six feet. The only roof was offered by a grove of tall conifers and beyond that, the sky. A fallen tree that lay over two of the boulders served effectively as a windbreak and would be handy for firewood in the bargain.

Even to Antonia's untrained eye, Ross had chosen well and already the heat from the fire was beginning to reach out to her, surrounding her.

"Careful, sweetheart," Ross said, taking her half-filled cup from her. Though he would have preferred that she eat, he wasn't surprised when she couldn't. He wouldn't push. Rest, at this point, was as vital. "Go back to sleep."

"I'm sorry. I didn't know I'd fallen asleep."

"Don't be sorry. You have every right to be sleepy. The altitude can do that. But, since you're awake, you should shed some of your clothing."

She was warm. Less than an hour ago, she'd never dreamed she'd be so warm again. The sweater went first, then the blouses, until she was down to the last. Sighing, she closed her eyes and leaned back again.

"What!" She bolted upright, the sleep clearing from her eyes as she stared at Ross. "What are you doing?"

"I'm taking off your shoes. What did you think?"

"Why?"

"Shh. Just sit back and relax, and you'll see." Her shoes were discarded and then her stockings. Taking her feet into his lap, Ross began to stroke them. At first gently, then with a firmer touch, working the tired muscles, soothing the strained tendons. Warming toes numbed both by the cold and from constantly jamming against the ends of her sneakers in their ever-downward trek. "Relax," he murmured as he paid particular attention to the instep. Squeezing and massaging each foot until the tingling ache of restored circulation turned to an ache of pleasure.

Then just as gently he began to blaze a slow trail up her legs. "Easy," he murmured when she tensed, his voice as soothing as his hands. "This won't hurt but a minute."

Her knotted calves protested beneath his ministrations, but as he'd promised, only for a minute. Skillfully, with tender purpose, he searched out every cramped fiber, and just as skillfully, just as tenderly, worked them free. As gnarled muscles responded, Antonia stopped thinking, feeling only the pleasurable stroke of his fingers against her flesh. A quiet groan whispered through her as the tangled tension of fear and worry unraveled into languid peace.

Through a fringe of lowered lashes, half waking, half sleeping, perhaps half dreaming, she watched him. In a gathering darkness broken only by the pale flickering glow of the fire, as he leaned to her his face was in shadow, the bold, rugged features hidden. But for her memory of deep-set eyes as cool and blue as a mountain lake, of sensual lips quick to smile but quicker still to mock, he was a stranger. One kinder and more gentle than the Ross she'd known.

The light flowed over his forearms, naked beneath up-turned cuffs. Power and strength seemed to emanate from them as his fingers danced down the length of her thigh. His head turned in profile to her, his shoulders flexed as he bent in concentration to his task. She felt herself drifting, mind as well as body mesmerized by the magic of his touch. Sleep clouded her vision, drawing her down with the weight of its demand.

She struggled against it, willing the lethargy away. Her eyelids fluttered, but refused to lift. Groaning softly she tried to rise. A hand touched her shoulder, exerting only the slightest counterpressure. A deep voice chided gently, "Sleep."

Sleep? When she was lost in the wilderness. When a blizzard threatened? When night was closing around her?

"Sleep, Antonia, I'm here."

Had she spoken aloud, or had he anticipated her thoughts? Did it matter? Did the wilderness? Or the blizzard? Or even the darkness? Did any of it matter when Ross, the stranger she never knew, was with her?

"We'll be safe here, I promise." Then ever softer, the last words she heard, "Sleep now, brave lady, sleep."

"Oohhh!" Pain sliced through her like a dagger, dragging her from a limbo that reached beyond mere sleep.

"What the devil?"

The muffled oath finished what pain had only begun. She was fully awake, and fully cognizant that it was Ross who cursed. Ross who held her in his arms carrying her from the hastily constructed resting place to a mélange of leaves and moss, silks and fur. A ridiculous concoction that out of necessity had been accepted almost casually as their communal bed.

But it was concern for Ross, not pain, nor that they would be sharing a bed again that had her frowning. He was regaining his strength. Every hour of every day saw the return of his stamina. But that he should carry her to bed was a foolish waste of his energy. Drawing a tentative breath, meaning to assert her own strengths, she gasped again. Her hands twisted in the fabric of his shirt, her forehead dipped to his shoulder. Rigid and tense, biting her lips against the whimper that caught in her throat, she waited for the hurt to recede.

Holding her, not daring to move, Ross stood as he had when he'd lifted her from the ground. Feet planted firmly, he let his body support her weight. With one arm tucked under her knees and the other encircling her body, he absorbed with his strength the impact of the racking shudder of unexpected pain. When she was still and the uneven staccato of her breathing steadied, he continued without speaking to the newly prepared bed, perfumed by fresh boughs of evergreen, adorned by its exotic and sensual coverlet of mink.

Carefully, grimly, he lowered her to the bed, caring little for the incongruity of its luxury. "Take off your blouse."

"What?" Leaning back with one arm bracing her, Antonia looked up at him as he knelt by her. Shock turned her eyes into wide, smoky pools in her pallid face.

"Take off your blouse," Ross said patiently. "I intend to see for myself what this fall that was nothing has done to you."

"There's no need." Her hand going instinctively to her blouse, Antonia shook her head, only to have Ross brush her fingers away as he dealt with the buttons.

"There's every need," he said almost absently as he moved with skillful ease from one tiny disk to the next.

Still caught in the unthinking numbness of surprise, Antonia heard herself saying inanely, "You do this very well."

"All buttons are the same, and I practice at it daily."

Made by another man, the sort who peopled her world, it would have been a lecherous remark, gloating, self-serving, suggestive. From Ross it was a simple commentary, a reminder gently given. "Your patients?"

"Yes." Whatever he might have added was cut short by a muttered curse as he brushed her blouse from her shoulders. Bands of chafed skin traversed the slope of her breasts and disappeared beneath a camisole that gleamed like ancient jade. An irritation not unlike it probably scored his own chest. Not enough to cause her outcry. Not nearly enough for this lady. Reaching to her hip, to tug the hem of the green garment from her jeans, he found her hand clutching his.

"What are you doing?" Her protest was fueled more by a need to keep hidden from Ross and herself any injury inflicted by stupid carelessness than for the sake of modesty.

Extracting his hand from her grasp, he slipped the slick fabric from her waistband. "I'm removing this little bit of nonsense. I want to see how badly your ribs are bruised." His voice dropped to a low guttural growl. "Or if they're broken."

"My ribs aren't broken."

"How would you know?"

"Because they've been broken before. I would know," she insisted. "And I wouldn't be so foolish as to ignore something potentially dangerous."

"Glad to hear it." He raised the lace-trimmed hem. When he realized she wore nothing underneath the camisole, rather than stripping it away as he'd intended, he stopped at her breasts, holding it there gathered in his palm, exposing the long, lean line of her torso.

Here are your BIG WIN Game Tickets potentially worth from $100.00 to $1,000,000.00 each. Scratch off the PINK METALLIC STRIP on each of your Sweepstakes tickets to see what you could win and mail your entry right away. (SEE OFFICIAL RULES IN BACK OF BOOK FOR DETAILS!)

This could be your lucky day - GOOD LUCK!

THE BIG WIN

TICKET 1
Scratch PINK METALLIC STRIP to reveal potential value of this ticket if it is a winning ticket. Return all game tickets intact.

LUCKY NUMBER

1P 925966

TICKET 2
Scratch PINK METALLIC STRIP to reveal potential value of this ticket if it is a winning ticket. Return all game tickets intact.

LUCKY NUMBER

4Y 925966

TICKET 3
Scratch PINK METALLIC STRIP to reveal potential value of this ticket if it is a winning ticket. Return all game tickets intact.

LUCKY NUMBER

3Q 925966

TICKET 4
Scratch PINK METALLIC STRIP to reveal potential value of this ticket if it is a winning ticket. Return all game tickets intact.

LUCKY NUMBER

9T 925966

FREE BOOKS

TICKET 5
We're giving away brand new books to selected individuals. Scratch PINK METALLIC STRIP for number of free books you will receive.

AUTHORIZATION CODE

130107-742

FREE GIFT

TICKET 6
We have an outstanding added gift for you if you are accepting our free books. Scratch PINK METALLIC STRIP to reveal gift.

AUTHORIZATION CODE

130107-742

YES! Enter my Lucky Numbers in THE BIG WIN Sweepstakes and when winners are selected, tell me if I've won any prize. If the PINK METALLIC STRIP is scratched off on ticket #5, I will also receive one or more FREE Silhouette Desire® novels along with the FREE GIFT on ticket #6, as explained on the back and on the opposite page.

NAME _____ 225 CIS AH76 (U-SIL-D-06/93)

ADDRESS _____ APT. _____

CITY _____ STATE _____ ZIP CODE _____

Book offer limited to one per household and not valid to current Silhouette Desire subscribers. All orders subject to approval.

PRINTED IN U.S.A. © 1991 HARLEQUIN ENTERPRISES LIMITED.

FOLD AND DETACH ALONG THIS DOTTED LINE—RETURN ALL GAME TICKETS INTACT.

THE SILHOUETTE READER SERVICE™: HERE'S HOW IT WORKS

Accepting free books puts you under no obligation to buy anything. You may keep the books and gift and return the shipping statement marked "cancel." If you do not cancel, about a month later we will send you 6 additional novels, and bill you just $2.24 each plus 25¢ delivery and applicable sales tax, if any.* That's the complete price, and—compared to cover prices of $2.99 each—quite a bargain! You may cancel at any time, but if you choose to continue, every month we'll send you 6 more books, which you may either purchase at the discount price . . . or return at our expense and cancel your subscription.

* Terms and prices subject to change without notice. Sales tax applicable in N.Y.

ALTERNATE MEANS OF ENTRY: Print your name and address on a 3"x 5" piece of plain paper and send to: Million Dollar Sweepstakes, 3010 Walden Ave., P.O. Box 1867, Buffalo, NY 14269-1867. Limit: One entry per envelope.

BUSINESS REPLY MAIL
FIRST CLASS MAIL   PERMIT NO. 717   BUFFALO, NY

POSTAGE WILL BE PAID BY ADDRESSEE

SILHOUETTE READER SERVICE
3010 WALDEN AVE
PO BOX 1867
BUFFALO NY 14240-9952

NO POSTAGE
NECESSARY
IF MAILED
IN THE
UNITED STATES

"Ross, there's really no need for this."

"Dammit, Antonia, hush. I've seen a woman's body before. I'm a yokel from the country," he reminded her of an opinion she'd expressed frequently, "not a fugitive from a monastery." Then, despite his remonstrance, as he glimpsed the underside of her creamy breasts, he asked grimly, "Why the hell didn't you wear a bra?"

"Why the hell didn't I wear a bra?" Her mimicking response was grated between gritted teeth. "I didn't wear a bra because I don't own one. Now if you would be so kind..." She gasped as his hands moved over her midriff, the arch of his fingers fitting the curve of her breast as it lay against her ribs.

"Does that hurt?"

"Yes," Antonia hissed as he probed and prodded.

"Is it sharp? Dull? Throbbing?" He didn't look at her, staring instead into the distance, seeing in his mind's eye the fragile bones beneath flesh as smooth as satin. There were no irregularities, no telltale lumps, no grinding bones, but he had to be sure. "Describe the pain."

"Dull," she said woodenly. "And only when I move carelessly."

Ross nodded, his gaze still unfocused as he concentrated on his examination. Their small campsite was astonishingly warm, but not warm enough to keep her from chilling. Gooseflesh rippled over her skin, and as he lifted his hand, tracing the line of lace as it dipped over cleavage and sternum alike, a turgid, satin covered nipple brushed against his wrist.

At this innocent, but intimate contact, Antonia grasped his wrist. "It's nothing, Ross. A bruise, perhaps, from my silly fall. But more than that, sore muscles as we should expect, from unaccustomed activity. It's only natural that I would be stiff and sore. Any unexpected move would exaggerate..." She shook her head, letting him follow her unspoken explanation to his own conclusion. "Tomorrow, on the trail, it should work out."

Ross agreed. For a moment he considered a cold compress for her ribs, but the bruise that had begun to discolor her side was only slight. They had been lucky this time, but she would be more tender over her ribs than she knew tomorrow. In fact she would hurt like the dickens at first, as she did tonight. He must see to it that her pack was lighter and didn't chafe.

Antonia shivered and he realized that the fire was dying down. Taking his hands from her, letting the camisole slide down to cover her, he turned to the fire, tossing on dry deadwood first to rekindle the blaze, then green sticks for longevity.

Satisfied with the quick flush of heat radiating through their small enclave, he turned back to Antonia. She had slipped into her blouse and was closing the buttons.

"Not yet." He took her hand away, and with the same finesse as before, bared her shoulders.

Antonia didn't waste words or energy with objection or challenge. For, she was discovering, it would truly be a waste. Ross would do exactly as he intended. And now he intended to hover as fiercely as he condemned.

From the nether regions of his makeshift pack he drew a small tube of cream. "Not exactly what I would prescribe, but better than nothing." Moving behind her he began to massage small amounts of it over her shoulders, sliding his fingers under threadlike straps of the camisole. First he lent his attentions to the irritation that blazed over bone and soft tissue of her chest. With a touch as light as a whisper he smoothed the cream over abrasion and bruise.

"Easy," he murmured quiet explanation as his hands and fingers ventured beyond the covering of her clothing. Without lingering, in one smooth, gliding move he stroked the substitute elixir over the swell of her breasts where the straps of her pack had lain. His touch was as gentle as a caress, as innocent as if she were one of his small patients. "Better?"

It was. The burning, achy sting she'd hardly noticed until now, until it was gone, had been cooled by Ross's stopgap medication. She was smiling now. "Much better."

Warmed by the rekindled fire, and more comfortable than she'd dreamed she could be, she simply accepted it when he began to knead the tightly strung tendons at her shoulders and neck. At first there was the flinching, shrinking hurt, but as he continued, finally, the ease into dreamy comfort. She barely noticed when he helped her into her blouse and settled her beneath the fur.

"Ross." She caught his hand in hers. "Thank you."

"For what, Antonia?" His voice was low, husky, but she didn't notice.

"For being so patient. So kind."

"I'm not sure I'm either."

"You are, you know," she insisted. As lethargy embraced her, she was aware of bone-deep weariness that even Ross's care could not remedy, yet without the frightening, breath-stealing panic so common before. The scent of evergreen drifted around her. The fur Ross tucked beneath her chin was familiar and comforting in an unfamiliar land. Antonia thought of her life, so carefully planned, of Jacinda her only friend. And of Ross, kinder than he would admit. Kinder than he knew. Far, far kinder.

Then she didn't think at all.

Long after she slept, Ross moved quietly around the camp, seeing to the fire, to their supplies, and mapping in his mind what he hoped would be an easier route down. When there was no more to do, he laid his weary body down by her.

"Ross?" His name was an unconscious murmur from the depths of sleep.

"I'm here." A promise made more times than she knew. It meant nothing, he told himself. Nothing that she called his name softly, nothing that she reached for him in her sleep.

"Nothing." He murmured as he drew her into his arms, remembering a single glimpse of her exquisite breasts, the feel of her skin beneath his finger, the brush of a nipple as delicate as a pearl against the tender flesh of his wrist.

"Ah, God, it means nothing," he declared as he laid his cheek against her hair, his lips teasing the dark, downy cloud.

"Nothing at all."

Seven

Ross looked over his shoulder, listening to the hushed, insistent murmur of Antonia's voice. As he tied a bright strip of cloth on a low-lying limb, one of hundreds he'd left to mark their trail for Dare, he smiled. A smile drawn in stark lines by the piercingly more frigid air that moved at their backs.

The downward flowing air was windless, thank God, and they were dry. Wind could sweep away the skin's natural shield of warm air and chill wet clothing. Windchill and hypothermia, a hiker's deadliest enemies. Though he was grateful for the merciful absence of wind, exhaustion coupled with wet and cold could be equally as deadly.

Antonia was coming to the end of her strength.

And the stillness itself was ominous.

Signs. Decisions. Risks. Neither could be avoided much longer. But for now a hunch, an instinct so vague he wasn't ready to put into words, had kept him moving. Moving and listening to Antonia talk to herself.

Actually she was reciting poetry, the lyrics of songs, lines from her last movie, lines from her next movie. Anything to keep her mind from the misery of the trail. By accident and sheer ingenuity, she'd stumbled on a practice common among experienced hikers. Daydreaming, or pretending, and the self-induced euphoria it created could dim even the most nagging discomfort.

More than once, as he'd tramped the forest, he'd rounded a bend or topped a rise, only to find more of the same, or worse ahead. The hardship was the price one paid when the wilderness beckoned. The euphoria was the mind's gift, a natural anesthesia. Ross had found it the most successful way to deal with a particularly difficult trek.

He dared not allow himself that luxury. Not today, or in the days before.

With Antonia only a few paces behind, he had to stay responsive and vigilant. He almost wished she were a whimperer, a whiner, or even a complainer. Then, at least, he would be warned when the breaking point was near.

But she didn't whimper, she didn't whine. She hadn't once complained. Neither was her way. Antonia's way was to duck her head, clench her teeth and cope. His task was to see to it that in coping, she didn't tap too deeply into her last reserve.

In the days following the crash and on the trail, she had honed down to sinew and muscles and pure grit. Sore muscles were hardening to meet the demand she put on her body. She had followed him obediently, but never meekly, deferring to his experience.

Under other circumstances the hike might have been enjoyable. Ross was discovering Antonia was an intelligent debater, an engaging conversationalist, a perfect listener.

A damn fine companion.

If conditions were better. But they couldn't be worse. Barely a day after they'd left the peak, the higher elevation had been engulfed in a frozen mist. Now that storm, stalled by the stagnant air, had begun to move, and it was moving down.

Signs pointed to the inevitable.

Snow.

He hadn't told her. He hadn't wanted to add to her troubles, but today by example he would ask her to walk farther, faster, longer. And she would. Without complaint, and if there were questions they would go unasked. Maybe, just maybe they could outrun the worst of it. Or maybe the hope born in his subconscious hours ago would become reality.

If neither came to pass? Making camp would be no problem. Neither would fire, nor warmth, nor water. Food was another matter. There was enough chocolate and coffee and tea and dehydrated goods to last a few more days.

If they were stranded for more than a while? He didn't like to think of the alternative. He wouldn't, not for another hour or two. Resolutely he blanked it from his mind.

Reassured of Antonia's endurance by her soothing mutter at his back, he stepped away from the brightly marked shrub. Listening to her voice, a sound as lovely as any he'd ever heard, he resumed his walk down the gloomy trail.

"It's spring! Almost April. It bloody well shouldn't snow in the south in spring! Not even in the higher elevations." The brogue acquired at his Scottish grandmother's knee slipped into Dare's speech as he slammed his open hand down on the table. Cutlery sent skittering by the force of the blow clattered against a plate still filled with food he hadn't touched.

From her place at his side, Jacinda closed her hand over his wrist. Grateful to have him back, even for one evening, she didn't speak, didn't offer platitudes for the agony that was tearing him apart.

Lifting her hand to his lips he kissed her fingers in reverence for this woman who spoke more with a silent touch than any other could in volumes. "He's alive, Jacinda, I know he is."

Jacinda only nodded as he released her abruptly.

Shoving his chair back, he spun away from the table. Striding to the window, he stared out at the cloudless sky. No snow in the foothills, only the cold.

"He's out there." He spoke to the night, his words hot against the frosty pane. "There in the darkness, waiting."

Slowly, rhythmically, Dare pounded on the window. Like the toll of a bell, his knuckles struck the pane. "He's waiting for me, and for his brothers." His shoulders stooped, his head bowed. "We can't find him, Jacinda."

"You will."

As always when he needed her, she was only a pace away. As always, no matter how her own heart might be breaking, her first thought was for Dare. Sliding her arms around him, resting her head against his broad chest, Jacinda listened as his grief poured from him.

"Ross is the best of us. He's the heart of the family. He made us what we are."

Jacinda murmured against his throat, tender wordless sounds. Her fingers tangled in his hair.

"He was eleven the first time I saw him. A rawboned, gangly kid with two babies in a rusty old wagon. He was my brother. The twins were my brothers. And I didn't know.

"*Our* father didn't want them, any of them. And if I didn't, then that was all right, too, Ross's sober look said. He'd manage. He had so far, he would still."

Dare's voice broke, he drew her nearer as if holding her closer would make a bad dream go away. His breath came in rasping shudders. "I'd had Gran, the security of the farm, the opportunity of an education. He'd lived a hand-to-mouth existence on the streets. His mother was dead, there was no home, no school. None of the normal things a kid deserves.

"His life was hunger and poverty and being dragged from city to city by John McLachlan." Dare spoke the name quietly with none of the hate he'd once felt. The name of a man long dead. "Ross doesn't talk about the women, but we're living proof they were second only to drink on John's list of weaknesses. I hope they were good to Ross. I think some of them must have been.

"Robbie and Jamie's mother stuck around for a while. Then one day she just disappeared, leaving them to live or die.

"With no help from our father, Ross kept them alive. He was a kid himself, half sick from malnutrition, but he did it. Can you imagine the hell of it? My life, in comparison, was paradise. Yet he didn't begrudge me anything. He only wanted a family."

"And to be wanted himself, Dare."

"I wanted him. The only honorable thing John ever did was to bring his sons to the farm, back to Gran. But Gran was dead, there was only me. *He* argued it should belong to her son, not me. But I couldn't let him have it, nor them.

"How could I not want a brother like Ross? How could I not be the man he wanted me to be? The man he already was?"

"Ross is an extraordinary man," Jacinda said. She'd heard the story before, but Dare needed to tell it. Needed for her to hear it. "All the McLachlan brothers are extraordinary."

Dare didn't acknowledge her tribute, his thoughts dwelt in the past. "After the cities, he was sure this was heaven. He never wanted to be anywhere but here. He'd found the family and the heritage he wanted. And the education his brilliant mind hungered for.

"There was never room for doubt in his future. He would be a pediatrician and practice in Madison. Nothing was more important. Except his brothers."

He stroked her hair and kissed her cheek. Lifting her face to his he murmured, "I have to find him, you know. Whatever it takes, however long."

"Yes." She knew. Dare was tired from too long on the search and too little rest, but Jacinda wouldn't try to stop him. Tomorrow, whatever the weather, he would be back at the search. If not in planes, then mapping strategy for when they could fly over the mountains again.

The slam of a door, the tramp of booted feet, signaled the twins were back from their part of the hunt.

Kissing her again, Dare released her and turned to his brothers with a look of hope. A glance at their grim faces sent it dashing to nothing.

"Not a trace." Robert Bruce, or Mac as he was known in graduate school at Georgia Tech, tossed his cap aside and rubbed his hand over his bearded face.

"David has taken Patrick and Rafe to Ross's place for the night," Jamie added, his own cap following his brother's. His face as in need of shaving.

"Raven and Jordana were here for part of the day. Keeping me company and playing with the babies," Jacinda told them. "It helped pass the time. They'll be back tomorrow, so it seemed more sensible that they should stay in town, rather than travel to and from the cabins in the valley." Going to the stove, she poured coffee for the younger McLachlans.

"Thanks, Teach." Jamie managed a grin. His eyes, red from strain and sleeplessness, crinkled at the corners as they had the first time she saw him. She could almost imagine none of this was happening, that he was still eighteen and still battling with Dare over his future. He would have been a magnificent lumberjack, but she thanked God he'd chosen the piano instead.

"Rob...I mean, Mac." She offered the second cup to the elder twin. "Sorry, I keep forgetting."

"Robert Bruce, Robbie, Mac. A name doesn't seem so important now." He took the cup and kissed her cheek. "What I'd like most right now is to hear Ross call me anything at all. Hey you, if it suited him."

"He will," Dare interjected. "And he might just add something in the bargain, for taking so long to find him."

Neither of them believed it. But Jacinda heard the positive tone. Suddenly it was *when* Ross was found, not if. The brothers gathered at the table, pushing untouched food aside, refusing the offer of more. Going to Dare's side, she listened to plans for the rest of the search.

"Patrick's bringing in more planes, and the forestry association will continue with their planes and foot search. That, in connection with the official investigation of the Civil Air Patrol, should turn up something. At least with Simon McKinzie on their case, they'll wish they had." Jamie sipped his coffee, then grimaced as it burned his chapped lips. "I don't think I'd want Simon 'on my case,' but I'd like nothing better than to have him on my side," he continued. "Who better than a government agent to ride herd on a government agency? An agent and a friend."

"With all due respect to Simon, a hundred planes won't find anything if they can't fly low enough to see the ground." This was the rage and frustration that was tearing Dare apart. "Snow," he muttered. "Why always in spring?"

"When it clears, Rafe wants to change the course of the search," Mac, or Robert Bruce, put in thoughtfully. "He isn't Patrick's CEO for nothing. He's sharp. His theory is there might have been some deviant wind currents running before the storm. If Ross was caught in one, he could've been thrown off course."

"Wind shear," Dare said almost conversationally. They knew what it could be. How lethal. "What's Rafe thinking?"

"He wants to study the weather maps for the day. Correlate it with Ross's flight pattern. Then, he admits frankly, he wants to speculate. To project possible happenings and conditions. He's asked me to help with that. He suggests my analytical engineer's mind might come up with an answer. He'd like to simulate some possibilities. He wants one plane to peel off from the routine search. One of Patrick's, of course."

"It could be dangerous, but if Rafe and Patrick are willing to take the risk, it's worth a try." Dare was already imagining for himself what could have occurred.

"I'm going with them." This from the elder twin.

"Me too." Jamie would not let a second brother go into danger without him.

"We'll all go," Dare decided. None of them could stay behind. For Ross's sake, but also because no McLachlan would ask friends to take risks they weren't willing to take themselves.

"When the weather in the mountains permits." Jacinda worried they might add bravado to tragedy.

"Only then, my love," Dare promised, though the waiting would be torture. Taking her hand in his, he drew her down to him. When she was nestled in his lap he kissed her. "Forgive me. I haven't forgotten that your dearest friend is up there somewhere with Ross."

She stroked his face, raking her fingertips over his unshaven cheeks. The stubble of a few days ago had become a soft, fledgling beard. "Ross will look after her. I have to believe that he'll keep her safe until you find them."

"Of course he will. Ross knows the land. He understands the weather. If there's shelter, he'll find it. If not, he'll create his own." With his rational observation the quieter twin, who was as much like Ross as Jamie was Dare, smiled at her.

"I know. Thank you." Then she touched his hand adding, "Thank you, Mac."

And on a ray of hope tangled irrevocably with his own genius, the ungainly name of a child was put aside by Jacinda in favor of the name of the man.

"Mac," Dare and Jamie said in unison, honoring the name with their coffee.

"Ross." Mac offered his own toast. "And Antonia. And to their safe return home."

"Ross and Antonia." Hope, unanimous, was spoken in unison.

There was nothing more to say. Food could wait, and the dishes. Rest was crucial.

Rest for the night. Hope for tomorrow.

Ross stopped as his path took him closer to the stream he'd been following for over an hour. He'd found this second rushing ribbon of water when his spirit was lowest. When he was ready to accept that they had lost the race and must call a halt for the day. Darkness had begun to fall and the trail was growing increasingly hazardous. Yet something, a premonition, hope, reinforced by the discovery of the stream, kept him pushing on.

He'd followed its shallow banks faithfully. Now, suddenly, the sharp incline of the land flowed into a level cove. The stream spilled in a fall over a jutting escarpment into a shallow half-frozen pool. It spilled again over a low earthen dam. Then strewn with ice it meandered through the flat land as if it had nowhere to go and no timetable to follow.

And there, across the water, in the shadowless twilight lay a trail worn by years of use. Shrugging out of his pack, letting it fall to the ground, Ross lifted his head, breathing in the scent that lay low over the land. Finally he let himself believe the truth that had been in the air for half the day. As the storm the day had promised began, he smiled.

"Smoke, Antonia," he murmured to her as if she were near rather than far beyond the reach of his voice. He laughed, a quiet rumble of elation and reprieve. "It was really smoke."

Somewhere down the twisting trail there was a camp or a cabin. "Not Dare," he cautioned himself, curbing a fantasy. "Too quiet, too contained for a search party."

Not Dare, not a search party, but he and Antonia weren't alone on the mountain. A human hand tended the fire that had burned throughout the day. Surely that hand would offer them shelter from the storm.

"Antonia." He turned as he called to her. In the last hour she'd lagged farther and farther behind, but now, because she was so tired, Ross knew her pace must be her own. She was standing, staring down at him from the top of the last incline. Stuffing his gloves into his pocket, with his hand outstretched, he went to lead her the rest of the way. "Come see what I've found."

He anticipated a jaunty riposte. A droll warning that the extra time on the trail had better be worth it. Instead she only bared her teeth in what didn't quite become a smile. In the last minutes since he'd glanced back to check on her she'd lost her gloves. But for too little time for the cold to do serious harm. Now her bare hand clutched at his like a vise, broken, unvarnished nails drove into his skin. Even in the dusk, beneath the cap pulled low over her brows, he saw that her face was drawn.

"What's wrong?" His eyes raced over her and before she could answer he saw. The heel of her shoe was rusty with stains of blood. Some of them old, some fresh. "Dear heaven! What have you done?"

He knew. He knew without taking off her shoe that he would find her heel raw, the skin worn away. With a bitter, angry oath he swept her into his arms and carried her down the slope. At a flat sheet of rock he sat her down and knelt at her feet.

Antonia sat as he placed her. Her shoulders slumped as he eased her pack from them. Her face was blank, uncomprehending, as her gaze followed his to her bloody foot.

Easing off her shoe, and then her socks, he inspected the damage. "How long?" he muttered impatiently. "How long have you been walking on this? Why didn't you tell me?

"Dammit, Antonia!" Her look of puzzled horror drew him up short. She hadn't told him because she didn't know. To keep the pace he'd set, to stay on her feet, she'd driven herself beyond thinking, beyond feeling. Dropping the shoe, he surged up to draw her to him. "Ah sweetheart, what have I done to you?"

Antonia clung to him, she was hardly aware that he spoke. Only that she didn't have to pretend anymore. Ross was real, he was warm. It didn't matter that he was angry, so long as he held her. Vaguely she wondered if there weren't something that needed an apology.

"Ross." His name was an exhausted whisper. "I'm sorry."

"Don't, sweetheart." Ross held her harder, tighter. "Don't make it worse for me."

"Have I?" She shook her head, trying to grasp a thought, then lost it. "I didn't mean to. I tried..."

"Hush, love." He moved a half pace away then crouched before her. Framing her face in his hands, he held her bewildered gaze with his. "You've done nothing wrong and you haven't made anything harder. I've done that quite nicely on my own. When you're rested, and can understand, I have some apologizing of my own to do. I'm not sure a lifetime would be long enough to make amends for what I've said. What I've thought." Tucking a wayward curl under her cap, his hand lingered at her throat. "But I'd like to try, if you'll let me."

Antonia touched his stubbled cheek catching a delicate crystal on her fingertip. "It's snowing."

"Yes." Taking her hands in his he cupped them against his lips, letting his breath warm them. Kissing her skinned knuckles he brushed his cheek against them as if willing away her hurt. "It's snowing, but it can't hurt us now."

"It can't?" Her face was still clouded by confusion. "How can that be?"

"Never mind." Pulling her sleeves over her bare hands, he bent to slide on her shoe, cursing himself for the pain he'd caused her. "There's something I need to do. I'll be gone for a short time. Will you be all right if I leave you?"

"You're leaving?"

"Only for a while, I promise." Snow was falling faster. Soon the ground would be covered. Already her clothing was dusted with white. "Stay here. Don't move." He touched her shoulder to brush away the snow and felt her shiver. "You're cold."

From the frame of his pack, where it was carried next to his body, he took the black fur. Wrapping her in it, he held the lapels closely to her chin. "I'll be back before you know it."

Turning he hurried to the stream and splashed across it. The ground was frozen, and once a wagon had traveled it, cutting deep ruts. But not in a long, long while. The trail was worn now only by human footsteps and the occasional animal. His own footing was unsure, but he had to go on, for with each jogging step the smell of smoke grew stronger.

One last twist of the trail and he saw it, wreathed with a gray mist around a tumbled down chimney barely taller than the roof of a tiny, clapboard shack. Perched precariously on rock pilings, its steps rotting, the porch sagging, the shack was beautiful. And through the murky glass of a crudely framed window a lantern flickered.

Ross stood at the gate of a gap-toothed picket fence, torn between the logic of knowing for certain what lay in store for them in the house, and by the intensifying need to return to Antonia. In the end he realized who, or what might wait for them beyond the fence was no longer critical.

Spinning away from the fence he knew he'd taken any choice from his own hands by pushing Antonia too far, too long.

The way back was more difficult. The darkness was deeper, the ground slicker. Unmindful that his feet were beginning to freeze, he waded the stream to her.

She was huddled as he left her, wrapped in fur and snow. Her head was down, her eyes closed. Whether in sleep or the first stages of hypothermia, he couldn't know. Diagnoses were of little use, for if it weren't the latter, it would be soon. Fatigue and exposure were slowly robbing her body of its ability to maintain its core temperature.

Antonia needed rest and shelter.

"She *must* have it. *Now.*" His words were muffled, their sound deadened by air rife with snow.

She scarcely responded as he lifted her from the rock. Only the soft sighing of his name and her hand curling at his nape communicated that she roused at all. Holding her Ross took her across the stream to the trail that led to their waiting haven. The trail, the canopy of trees, the breath he drew, were shrouded in white.

The icy crystals fell on his face and clung to his lashes blinding him. With each step the way grew worse, the veil of white more impenetrable. Just when he feared he'd lost his way, that by some miscalculation he'd zigged when he should have zagged, a flame blazed through the darkness.

Muttering regrets to the owner, he kicked the frail gate aside and crossing the few feet to the house, climbed ice-encrusted steps. With the toe of a soaked shoe he tapped at the door and waited with more patience than he felt. When there was no response, no sign of life, he tapped again.

A shadow flitted at the window, the flame in the lantern wavered.

Stepping back, he let himself be seen by whomever peered out at him. In a tone meant to assure, he called out, "We mean you no harm, but, please, we must have shelter."

The little house tucked in its tiny haven was still.

Ross listened to the stillness, hearing only the patter of snow against snow. Surely even a creature so reclusive he'd chosen to live in such utter isolation wouldn't turn them away.

Ross waited.

Only the flame moved, swirling and dancing in the lantern's glass sphere.

"I know you're there. I've been following the smell of the smoke from your chimney for hours."

The only answer was the whisper of the snow. *Pat, pat, patting* with grating monotony.

"Open the door." Ross fought sudden rage at the stony cruelty that lurked so silently behind the door. He'd never in his life intruded where he was not wanted. But now he would, if he must. "I won't go away. I can't." Then in a reasonable tone that belied the threat of his words, he called out, "It won't do either of us any good if I have to kick this door in."

Nothing.

"Dammit! Open..."

A hinge creaked. The door swung open. Ross had no idea what he expected. A shaggy hermit? A hulking throwback to the days of mountain men the likes of Boone, Sevier, Jackson?

Nothing could have surprised him as much as the ancient woman who stood in the portal of the open door.

"No need to swear, young man. Won't make these old bones move even a mite faster." Crossing her arms over the barrel of the shotgun she leaned against, she nodded her silver topknot to Antonia. "Your friend's plumb tuckered out, I guess."

"I guess." Biting his tongue, Ross curbed his impatience. This tiny myrmidon had proven she would not be hurried.

"Walked a ways, did you?" Dark, snapping eyes inspected him. Inspected the little of Antonia that was visible.

"More than a ways."

"Cold?"

"Numb."

"In need of some warm vittles?"

Ross simply nodded. The snow was pelting his back. His feet were blocks of ice, yet the chivalry instilled in him by Dare wouldn't let him push past her. Not yet.

Deliberately she regarded him. Head cocked to the side, her dark eyes squinted from a wrinkled face that had once been striking, if never beautiful. Finally her judgment was made. "You have a decent countenance."

"I would hope that I do. I try to be."

"Ross?" Antonia stirred in his arms, her head moving restlessly against his coat. "Who...?"

"Shh," he soothed her, laying his cheek against the cap that covered her hair. "Everything's all right, Antonia."

"Ross? That's your name?" Again eyes as black as soot probed his. "And this woman, Antonia, is your woman?"

"My name is Ross McLachlan," he volunteered. "And, yes, she's my woman." It seemed simpler this way. "Yes," he repeated in a voice as soft as the pat of the snow, "Antonia is my woman."

"Then, Ross McLachlan, why are you dawdling out there on the porch letting your woman get colder and hungrier?" Setting the shotgun aside she slanted him a look. "In case you're wondering, at ninety-two, I can still shoot out the eyes of a squirrel."

"Believe me, I wouldn't doubt it for a minute."

"That don't mean I'm going to shoot you."

"I sincerely hope not."

Incredibly she chuckled. "Not afraid of the devil himself, are you, Ross McLachlan? I like that in a man. I imagine Miss Antonia does, too." Then, without waiting for an answer, she gestured impatiently. "Come in. Come in. 'Tisn't a fit night for man nor beast, much less handsome scalawags and their ladies."

Older than Methuselah, skinnier than a willow switch, she turned away to lead him into her house. Ducking under the low door frame, Ross followed, and stepped back in time.

Halting just inside the door, he stared at the compact interior. There were two rooms, the larger, where he stood, was obviously the living space. On one side a bed, a nightstand and a chair stood against the wall. On the other was a wood stove for cooking, a table and chairs and a nearly empty wood bin. A rocker with a half-finished quilt folded in its seat was drawn to the side of a fieldstone fireplace that dominated the center of the room. In it blazed the fire whose life-giving smoke had guided him here.

There was no telephone, no electricity. By modern standards even the essentials were missing. But unlike its crumbling outside, the room where he stood, with its exquisite handmade furnishings, was utterly charming.

They would be comfortable and warm, and welcome here.

Aware of the old woman's patient, birdlike stare, he forced his frozen face into a smile. "I didn't mean to frighten you, Mrs...."

"Cade. Orelia Cade." She folded her arms over her flat

bosom. "And you didn't frighten me. Wouldn't live way up here alone if every little thing was going to frighten me."

"No, ma'am. Of course not."

With a brisk nod the old woman waved him to the fire. "Come warm yourselves by the fire, while I see to beds for you. Your woman's already drifted off again."

Ross glanced down at Antonia's still face, her lashes lay like dark shadows against her cheek. "Yes, ma'am, she has. But we don't want to inconvenience you. A pallet by the fire will do."

"For you, maybe, but not for this pretty little thing." Orelia gestured to the bed. "She'd sleep best here."

"It's kind enough of you to offer us shelter, Mrs. Cade. We couldn't take your bed."

"Nonsense!" Orelia had thrown open the door to a smaller room, gesturing toward it. "This was the room I shared with my husband for seventy odd years, I welcome an excuse to sleep in it again."

Ross knew when he was outmaneuvered and this small drill sergeant had every angle covered. "Then when we've seen to Antonia, I'll gather some wood and build a fire so the room will be warm for you."

"Now that would be a real kindness."

Later, as he lay in his nest of quilts by the fire, Ross listened to the restless sounds of Antonia stirring in her sleep. Beyond the closed doors, Orelia Cade snored quietly.

Two women, one old, one young, each strong in her own way. And he owed his life to both of them.

Eight

The light was radiant, golden, casting dark-limned images in shadowy relief against her eyelids. Subtle scents tickled her nose in strange and familiar medleys. Rose and verbena, sassafras and ginger, apples and mint, linseed oil and beeswax. Charming fragrances. Tantalizing, comforting. Then she remembered, fragrances from the past.

A rocker creaked, a low, quavery voice hummed "Rock of Ages" a half note off-key. Savoring a glorious feeling of safety and comfort, Antonia stretched with a lazy purr and opened her eyes.

"Well now, look at you! Awake at last." A gentle voice. The voice of a stranger, yet as hauntingly familiar as the scents. "Land sakes!" The childish delight was expressed so immediately, Antonia had no time to react. "Aren't you a pretty thing with your eyes like silver?"

Peering through lashes that fringed her weighted eyelids, Antonia regarded the ancient woman peering back at her. When a gnarled, blue-veined hand stroked her forehead, brushing her hair carefully back from her temple, it seemed natural.

"A mite muddled yet? I'd 'spect you would be." Again the comforting hand, the skin like old parchment stroking Antonia's. "Just rest a mite. Waking comes slow to the senses when you've slept for days."

"For days?" Antonia frowned, trying to remember.

"Two to be exact. Two days since your man brought you out of the storm."

The storm! It had been snowing.

"Ross!" Antonia lurched upright. As the quilt fell away from her breasts she discovered she was naked, but she didn't care. All she cared about was Ross. "Ross?" She looked frantically around the small cozy room. "Where is Ross?"

"Hush now, he won't be taking it kindly if I let you work yourself into a lather." For all their swollen arthritic knuckles and crooked fingers, there was wiry strength in the grip that leaned her back. "Won't take it kindly of himself, either, now that you've finally waked up and he's not here. Nosiree, hasn't left your side, until today. Wouldn't now, but he felt he had to. Something about marking a trail for his brother."

Antonia closed her eyes, remembering the plane and the stony clearing. The trail down the mountain that seemed to go on forever. Snow, cold, fear. Her strength and her resolve spiraling down to wretched defeat and the world becoming a blur of jumbled vignettes. Ross's arms around her. The beat of his heart beneath her cheek. The sway of his step. Trees like a canopy over their heads. A pale, wavering light falling through the window of a tumbledown cabin. His voice calling out. Gentle, rising in anger, gentle again.

Then suddenly there was no snow, and she was wonderfully, luxuriously warm. She had slept, and while she slept, voices and scents from the past and the present wove themselves into the tapestry of her dreams.

Footsteps. The fire crackled and the clatter of glass rang musically through the room. A new scent, wonderfully delicious, wafted on still air. More footsteps. The solid thud of wood against wood. Antonia realized she wasn't dreaming again when the old voice spoke with a chuckle.

"Drowsy, or just getting your bearings?"

"A little of both, I think." Antonia pulled the quilt closer under her chin, her gray stare unfocused.

"Then this should perk you right up." She set a steaming cup on the bedside table. "Sip a bit, then we'll get you prettied up for your man's return."

From a wooden chest she lifted a bundle. Sitting on the side of the bed, from folded tissue she lifted a long gown of pale rose-tan cotton lawn, with rows of creamy, delicately crocheted lace. "I knew the minute I saw those gray eyes as shiny and pretty as a storm-washed sky that this would be special on you."

With the quilt clutched to her breasts Antonia sat up, spellbound by the elegant creation. "I've never seen anything like it." Touching the fine cloth, she traced a line of tiny stitches. "You made this?"

The pale, wrinkled cheeks were flushed with color. "It was intended for the wife I hoped my son would bring home some day. Some things were just not meant to be."

"It's lovely—" Antonia touched her hand "—but I couldn't wear it."

Black eyes regarded her solemnly. "It'll be a tad short, but you've got a nice turned ankle. Won't hurt to show a bit of it. The gathers at the neck and the full bodice should accommodate the rest of you." Rubbing the lace between thumb and forefinger, she looked away. "I'd count it a favor if you could see your way clear to wearing it."

Antonia realized suddenly how much it meant to the old woman. "Then I'd be honored to wear this beautiful gown." Folding the misshapen hand in hers she said with regret, "Forgive me, I can't even thank you properly. I don't know your name."

"Orelia." A smile lighted her features, and traces of the handsome woman she had been were visible. "Orelia Cade."

"And I'm Antonia."

"Well, now." Orelia stood dusting invisible wrinkles from her apron. "We have lots to do, but I think your man will be a while yet. I heard the ax over by the stream just before you woke. Figured he saw the tree down at the dam and decided to chop it for firewood after he marked the trail.

"It's a fine man who can't let good wood go to waste. So far your man has the makings of the finest."

"He's not . . ."

"He'll be a while, but that don't mean we don't have to hurry." Cocking her head to the side, she studied Antonia. "What to do first?" Then, tapping her head with a finger as if she couldn't believe she was so dense, she exclaimed, "A bath! Of course you'll want an all-over bath. We've sponged you in bits and pieces, but it's not the same."

"We?" Antonia managed one beat late. That Ross had seen her and touched her body without her knowledge sent a flush of heat through her.

"Truthfully it was mostly me. But your man took care of your face." The light dimmed in her bright gaze. She shook her head, her attention on the healing, crimson welt at Antonia's temple. "A pity, but it could've been worse. He was careful of it when he combed and braided your hair." She'd crossed to a cabinet and was drawing out an old oak tub. Sitting back on her haunches she looked back at Antonia. "He likes to braid your hair. Says it keeps him from tangling in it in his sleep and pulling at your hurt."

"In his sleep?" Antonia was a little dazed, but Orelia was too busy to notice. It had seemed natural to curl in Ross's arms after the crash and on the trail. Then it had been necessary, a matter of survival. But now?

"No time for daydreaming, girl," Orelia scolded. "I set the water to boil a spell ago. Once I pour it in the tub and add cold water from the well by the porch, it should be just right. All that's left is you, and we'd better get cracking."

"I suppose we'd better." One last, quick sip of the warm drink, and Antonia rose from the bed. Wrapped in the quilt she went to the waiting tub.

"And this one?" Antonia pointed to the curling, yellowed photograph pasted on the stark black pages of the album resting on her knees. She was sitting in a rocker before the low-burning fire. Tiny glasses perched on her nose, one bare, healing foot was tucked at the laddered crosspiece of her chair.

Orelia looked up from her tatting, her flying fingers still. "That one was my Lon."

"Your husband?"

Orelia nodded, her mouth pursed against the sadness in her eyes. "His name was Alonzo, but to me he was Lon."

"He was a handsome man, and talented." Antonia gestured to the plain, but handsome furniture that Orelia kept polished with linseed oil she made from flax. Antonia had seen more ornate furnishings, but none finer.

"He was that, and a good, hardworking man with it," Orelia agreed.

"Afternoon, ladies." Ross stood in the doorway. His jacket had been discarded, the buttons of his shirt were missing or torn open. The sleeves were rolled back to his elbows, and the gleam of sweat shone on his forehead. In his arms lay a stack of wood for the stove, the fruit of his afternoon of labor.

"Ross!" The album tumbled to the floor as she twisted in her seat to face him.

"No one else." The women had been so engrossed in their conversations, neither had heard him come in, affording him the opportunity to watch Antonia without her knowledge. Dusk had begun to fall, and the oil lamps were burning. In their light, she seemed to glow and her hair rippled over her shoulders looking like burnished ebony. Shiny and clean and faintly damp. The heat of the fire and the rose-tan of the quaintly beautiful gown she wore brought color back to her cheeks. With each move, as she'd turned the pages of the great book, fragile lace drifted in a pale, creamy mist over her breasts and her wrists.

As she looked up at him, the flush heightening in his presence, she was lovelier than Ross had ever seen her. So lovely it was painful when he realized with a shock how badly he wanted to touch her.

Flexing his fingers over the wood, scarcely noticing the splinter he drove into his finger, he nodded and muttered his greeting, "Mrs. Cade, Antonia." Striding across the room, ever aware that Antonia watched him, he filled the wood bin then stood in the shadows wondering what it was he saw in her face. Concern? Gratitude? Pleasure?

"Warm cider?"

Drawn from his thoughts he looked vaguely down at Orelia.

"Cider?" She offered him a cup, aromatic steam rising from its rim. "I know it's already warming outside, but there'll be a chill in the night air, as long as the snow lies this deep."

"Thank you." Ross took the cup, his gaze returning to Antonia as he sipped from it. She hadn't moved, her gaze hadn't wavered. He had to touch her, had to feel the warmth of her rosy cheek beneath his palm. Setting the cup on what Orelia called the fire board over the fireplace, he crossed to Antonia.

Standing over her he waited for her to look up at him. Waited for the wealth of her hair to fall down her back like a tempting veil.

"Ross."

Just his name, no more, and the blinders he'd worn for days fell away. He heard in her voice, and saw in her eyes none of the innocent compassion that let Antonia hold him as he thrashed in the throes of delirium. None of the desperation that made sleeping in each other's arms on the trail a sexless need for life-giving warmth. None of the sleepy unease that had him leaving his pallet by the fire to slip into her bed each night, telling himself he meant only to hold her, to ease her restlessness so she would not wake Orelia.

With his name and a look, every lie he'd told himself lay in ashes. He wanted her. He had long ago on the mountain, on the morning he'd wakened, for the first time fully alert and cognizant, in her arms. Perhaps he'd wanted her from the moment he'd met her. An explanation for the strange animosity he'd had to work so hard to preserve over the years. Protective bias, stripped away by the simple truths of survival.

None of it seemed of any consequence. Neither goals nor ambitions. Not what had been and would be again. In this tiny cabin there were no differences, no past, no future. There was only the desire he saw reflected in her face.

Of its own volition his hand curved around her nape, his fingers tangling in her hair. The scent of flowers rose from it in tiny little ebbs with the rush of her pulse. Her glittering eyes, turned to smoky amethyst by the fire and the rose of her cheeks, returned his look levelly. If he'd any doubts there would be none now.

"I missed you." Her voice was low and soft, and he almost forgot that Orelia was watching. He almost didn't care.

"I know." He knew, dear Lord, he knew. He might try to fool himself that this awareness had come out of the blue, but he would be lying again. Once he saw that her sleep was normal, healthy sleep, it was this, the need in him, and the fear that it would find no answer in her, that kept him away from the cabin all day. The ache of it had thrown him into a frenzy of chopping and splitting and stacking wood. More wood than would be needed in months. Still he'd driven himself, until he was bathed with sweat and every muscle protested.

In the cold, crisp air, stripped down to a tight khaki shirt and jeans, his punished body burned with desire for her. And in the end, desperation had driven him to bathe in an ice-encrusted stream.

All of it had been futile. He was here now, touching her, feeling the silken skin under his fingers, needing more. And, incredibly, seeing the same needs, the same remnants of fear in her eyes.

Dear heaven! How? he wondered, his fingers tightening possessively in her hair, how could she ever be afraid he wouldn't want her?

Watching from her place by the wood stove Orelia smiled and furtively closed the damper she'd just opened. There would be no need to warm biscuits and stew for the evening meal.

"You know—" folding a hand over her mouth, she stifled an imaginary yawn "—it's been a long day and I'm really not hungry for supper. If no one minds, I think I'll just go on to bed. There's biscuits if you get hungry." Neither Ross nor Antonia heard. Orelia chuckled. "Well, I don't suppose you'll be needing food. At least for a while."

Going to a tall cabinet she called a chifforobe, she collected a set of tarnished silver candle holders and pure white tapers wrapped in tattered tissue paper. Lighting them with a broom straw brought flaming from the fire, she placed them on the table before the window. Then smiling at the success of the ambience they created, and with a pleased glance at her guests who had forgotten her, she took the lamp and left them.

Her footsteps had faded behind the closed door of her bedroom before Ross looked away from Antonia. "Orelia?"

"She's gone." Antonia stroked his hand as it rested at her shoulder.

"It's early. She hasn't had dinner."

"I don't think she cares."

"Surely she's not that tired."

"No, but she's answered a thousand questions today."

"Questions?"

"My questions about you. I had to know if you were well."

Ross touched the yellowing bruise at his forehead, smiling wryly. Obviously he had recovered, or nearly so. He'd forgotten the concussion and any lingering effects of it completely in his zealous labor.

Seeing the gesture, interpreting it as affirmation of Orelia's assurances, Antonia drew a relieved breath. "If that catechism wasn't enough, there was more. Where were you? When would you return? I must have asked the same questions hourly, but she answered again and again. More than that, she tolerated my wandering attention as I watched the door, waiting for you."

Suddenly unnerved by her own honesty, Antonia bent to pick up the album. Ross was there before her, kneeling at her feet, taking the book from her clumsy fingers, setting it aside on the table by her chair. His silent gallantry restored her courage. Touching his face she skimmed her fingers over the growth of beard he'd trimmed into a passable Vandyke. His skin had been bronzed by his day in the sun and its reflection on the snow. His eyes were bluer, his teeth whiter. The tanned skin shading into the darker beard was wickedly handsome. Ross, her modern-day rogue.

"You thought I didn't know when you came in." She murmured, biting back a gasp as he turned his head lazily, grazing her fingertips with his lips. "But I knew. How could I miss the footsteps I'd waited all day to hear?"

"As I'd waited all day to come to you, my brave lady." Without rising Ross traced a line over her temple above the healing cut half hidden by her hair.

"Will you braid my hair now?"

"Leave it loose. I want your hair loose."

Antonia covered her temple as the memory of his touch lingered. "Because it hides this? The scar offends you?"

"No." A terse response, muttered hoarsely, gruffly, without explanation or qualification.

Remembering the pleasure he'd drawn from braiding her hair, and Orelia's assertion that as she slept, caring for her hair had been his ritual, Antonia wondered what had changed.

Seeing her bewilderment he climbed to his feet, drawing her up with him. "I won't braid your hair. For days I've wanted to feel it winding around me, binding me to you as I made love to you. I *am* going to make love to you, Antonia." His fingers twined in her hair in tender emphasis. "Here. Now."

The room had grown darker as the sun made its slow descent beyond the mountain. The light of creamy candles glinted in her eyes, over the rise of her bosom, and the shadowed décolleté of borrowed finery. She stood utterly still before him, her shoulders straight, her gaze meeting his. "Will it be love, Ross?"

Releasing her he stepped back. "Would it frighten you if it were?" Now it was his turn to go starkly still, waiting for the most important answer he would ever have.

She was silent, her head bowed. The sweet intoxicating scent of the candles mingling with her own, rose to him. Erotic, tantalizing, enchanting. Her breasts lifted in a long shudder. Their peaks taut against smooth lawn were shadows within shadowy folds. When she lifted her face, her eyes were bright.

"It would frighten me only if it weren't." Her voice was a ragged undertone, avoiding the word love as if it were part of a make-believe world. As if by saying it she would shatter the magic that shielded them from reality.

"Don't be afraid, Antonia. Not of me. Not because it isn't real." Hooking his little finger in her hair at the level of the raw scar, trailing through it, smoothing it, he coiled the curling ends over lace that lay against her breasts. "We're here. We're alive, and nothing could be more real than this." Tilting her chin with a knuckle, he met her look gravely. "I love you. I think that I've loved you for a long time. Fool that I am, it took nearly losing you to make me see.

"Hear me, Antonia." He was suddenly fierce. "I have loved you. I do love you. I will love you. For now. Forever."

The flush of her cheeks drained away. Her eyes glittered like new silver. She tried to speak and couldn't find her voice. Her arms opening to him, wanting him, needing him, said enough.

Ross stepped into her embrace, drawing her to him. Crushing her breasts to his chest, he felt the hard, delicate nipples thrusting through folds of lawn, pressing against heated flesh bared by his open shirt. But as he bent to kiss the curve of her shoulder and the hollow of her throat, even that fragile barrier was too much.

Antonia's head was thrown back, offering him access to her body, and as he slid his hands beneath the lace to caress her, she shivered. He slipped the gown from her shoulders, watching as it drifted down, and down, cleaving to a nipple, catching at the bend of her arms.

He muttered an oath in frustration. He wanted to see her.

Reveling in his touch, she clung to him, her hands at his shoulders to steady herself. He smelled of cold, crisp air, of clear water and sunshine. His body was nearly bare, the shirt with its torn and dislodged buttons hid little of his deeply muscled chest and corded midriff. In the half-light of the tiny room, power radiated from him. This strong and brawny mountain man. This tender man.

He said he loved her; the words were sweet music to her ears. But it was the look in his eyes, sweeter than any words, that was music to her heart. He spoke of time, but time had stopped for Antonia. Yesterday and tomorrow were no longer real.

Taking his hands in hers, she lifted each palm to her lips, kissing the hollow that had cradled and caressed her. Then, deliberately, she released him. The fire was at her back, its muted brilliance rimming her body in a scintillating halo. She lowered her arms, letting the gown fall away.

Her moment of hesitation had passed. Antonia waited for him. That he loved her and wanted her was enough. "We're here," she murmured giving back his words. "We're alive. Nothing could be more real than this."

If Ross hadn't been lost before he would've been then. With no thought to tomorrow he shrugged his shirt aside and drew her back to him. As her breasts brushed against his nakedness, he kissed her. A kiss too demanding, too possessive, too passionate, to be gentle.

Antonia shivered from the onslaught. He was stroking her, finding the secret places that yearned for his touch. He was her lover, claiming her for his own. No thought occurred to resist his possession. She didn't think at all as her own needs broke free of rigid little rules and tidy absolute boundaries set a lifetime ago. Like a tide, desire washed them away.

His kisses burned, scorching a trail from her jaw to the hollow of her throat. To her breasts. His beard teased her skin, his tongue was rough sand against the nipple. His suckling robbed her of the last of her strength.

"No more." She swayed, her hands grasping at his hair. "No more."

Ross lifted his head, stunned by the innocence of her cry. Didn't she know? On her face he saw heavy-lidded sensuality and wonder. The same wonder he'd discovered in himself. Was it only that he heard? Only that he saw?

"Ross."

"Shh. I know, love. I know. It's too much, too wonderful." He led her to the bed, releasing her only long enough to shed the last of his clothing. When he returned to her she was standing as he'd left her. As she had at every turn she had grown more beautiful in his eyes. Like a butterfly gradually emerging from its chrysalis, the alluring couturier's darling had become the enchanting ragamuffin.

And the ragamuffin with all her compassion and her courage had become the most beautiful of all. A woman, innocent and beguiling, cloaked in candlelight. Drawing her down with him to the goose-down mattress, he promised, "But there is more, sweetheart. So much more that we've just begun."

Something changed in him then, Antonia sensed but did not understand. There was more, yet less. He was more demanding, more possessive, more maddening. Yet every move was less and less hurried. Deep, restive passion seethed in his caress, his kiss. And all the while each stroke of his fingers and brush of his lips seduced her completely, exquisitely. Each time she thought he was wrong, that there could be no more, his hands and mouth journeyed to new places.

And there was more. She was spiraling up and up, something in her coiled even tighter as delicious inertia turned bone and sinew to molten fire. She wanted to flow around him, enveloping him, staying the hands and nimble fingers that were demons of this madness.

Liar!

Dear heaven! Yes, she lied. She never wanted him to stop. If this was madness, she never wanted to be sane again.

This honesty was power. Power that swept away timid restraint. Suddenly she understood that she could take him with her into this rapture, that her touch could leave him breathless as she was breathless, that her kiss could make him tremble as she trembled. The magnificent joy that rippled through her was hers to give as well as receive.

Flowing with him, with firelight sculpting the merging curves and angles of their bodies, she touched and explored, kissed and caressed. With the delicate scent of Orelia's candles drifting around them in a sultry mist, she bound him to her with her hair.

Tighter, closer, sweeter. Breasts brushing in delighted teasing over his bare skin. Thighs slid against thighs, legs entwined. Then, shuddering kisses with tongues feasting.

More.

For Antonia.

More.

For Ross.

Candles guttered, snuffing out. His world was filled now with only her scent. The scent of roses mingling with wood smoke. Their bodies glittered and shone, slick with the heat of desire. Ross lifted her above him, her body cradled between his thighs. The black fall of her hair rippled over him as his eyes held hers. Then slowly his look moved over her mouth, down her throat. Half rising to her he kissed the pulse that throbbed there. And when she arched her breasts against him, he took the nipple in his mouth. One and then the other, until she was shaken by tremors, and her cry became his name.

A man possessed, he turned with her, rising over her. He had no idea it could be like this. He hadn't expected that her need would intensify his, that her pleasure would be his.

Love, not lust.

The difference he hadn't expected.

Hadn't understood.

Brushing from her face the black, silken strands that had bound him more surely than any shackles, he called her name. Only her name. "Antonia."

He needed to see her face, needed to hear his name on her lips when he claimed her as his. "My name," he whispered against the slow rise of her breast. "Say my name."

With a breath caught and held, on the crest of rending pain forgotten in wonder, she whispered, "Ross." And then, "My love."

Ross sat in the dark, embers of the fire turning from crimson to gray as he watched her sleep. So much he'd questioned was clear now. The untried kisses, the unskilled hands, the innocence. Perhaps he should have been surprised or even shocked, but he wasn't.

Antonia Russell was an extraordinarily attractive and talented woman. A citizen of a world that accepted sex and lust as routine. A success in a profession that too often demanded innocence as its price. There had been lovers on the screen, lovers on the stage. Tabloids and newspapers blazoned the hottest and "latest breaking" news of her newest romance, naming names of off-screen lovers, in bold, black headlines. Always from that unimpeachable source. Someone who *knew!*

Wouldn't that unimpeachable source be stunned if he or she really knew? Wouldn't the avid reader be disappointed to discover it was simply gossip, part of a make-believe world?

Would they believe? Could they? Ross felt the sweet stab of truth, savoring it. Awed by it. There had been no lovers before him. No love.

Leaning forward in his chair he gathered up a quilt that spilled over the floor. With cautious care he tucked it around her naked shoulders, to guard against the chill that crept through the room. His hand tarried at her breast. Her heart beat a steady rhythm beneath his fingertips as he searched her face, trying to remember the woman he'd thought her.

He couldn't find that creature. She hadn't existed, except in tabloids. And in his own defensive mind. Now those pitiful defenses were gone. Fallen, like dominoes, one after the other. He could never resurrect them. He wouldn't try.

Antonia held his fate in her hands. Their future was hers to choose.

Stirring, she murmured his name, and in sleep her fingers twined with his. Ross sighed, relieved all over again that her sleep was natural. Only fatigue. That, too, was natural. The normal, healthy reaction of a strong mind and body to physical exhaustion. The panic she'd tried to hide at the christening, the sweaty, hyperventilation brought on by emotional and mental stress, hadn't occurred again.

The body's needs were easily recognized, more easily met than the insidious needs of the mind. Physical exhaustion was more readily accepted and addressed. Mental exhaustion, the common but darkest secret of the strong, couldn't and wouldn't be admitted until cloaked in face-saving terms. Burnout. A trendy label for an old malady.

Bizarre as it was, the crash, the struggle for survival, had been the change Antonia needed. One demand replaced another. The more critical the demands, the stronger she'd become.

Time would tell, but Ross the physician believed she would go back to her make-believe world a magnificent woman. "You picked a hell of a way to resolve your problems, sweetheart." He touched her cheek, feeling the sweep of her lashes against his finger. "And I?" he wondered aloud. "How do I resolve loving you?

"Physician heal thyself?" Some things were impossible.

A sound rumbled beyond the mountain. The muttering growl of spring. The awakening tyrant, who could be as cruel as she was kind, shifting, changing. Ross shivered with the warning and from the cold. Rising, he went to the fire. With the logs he'd stacked against the hearth, he fed the smoldering ashes. A blaze licked at dry tinder. Soon it danced in mesmerizing flame, sending comfort through the room.

Ross lifted his hands, warming them as he stared into the fire, remembering. The heat, the tangle of sensations, the passion of the woman who had been his in the circle of its light.

The drowsy tyrant rumbled again.

Thunder.

Spring was not done with her tricks. Soon it would rain, melting the snow. And Dare would come.

Ross stood, his face grim, his bleak eyes turning to the window and the night that had fallen. "But not yet." The rain was far, far in the distance. There was still time. Time that was theirs alone.

When he went to her, stepping over bare floors and ancient rag rugs, his body was aching with his need of her. As he slid under the covers it was lover, not physician, who took her in his arms.

As if it were natural to wake with his lips at her breasts, she murmured her welcome and reached for him, stroking his jaw, fingers curling for a moment in his beard. If he'd wondered about curbing his passions, he knew with her touch that he needn't. Her memories, like his, were the only prelude needed.

A flicker of lightning enhanced the firelight and he saw the glow of desire on her face. Beneath the languid layers of sleep, he felt the silent, delicate quickening, the hunger. Her breath whispered over his shoulder, her kisses brushed his skin. Her fingers fluttered over the hard muscularity of his back, drawing him down to the center of her.

Ross muttered a soft desperate sound at the intimate contact, but her furor was first to break, her body first to demand. Searching for his mouth, her fingers digging furrows in his back, her hips arched, her body undulated to receive him.

The last worry for the rain was gone, the last languor of sleep. Sleek bodies merged clouding reason. Desires intensified with each caress, each arc of bodies. No words were spoken but the room sang with their lovemaking. Soft sounds. Hoarse, inarticulate murmurs. Sighs caught back in marveling gasps. The cry of surrender. Passion's song, quieted at last by release.

Long, hushed moments later Antonia spoke her first coherent words. "I didn't understand." Searching for the words to tell him what he'd given her, she clung to him, her eyes were closed. Slick with sweat, her body molded his. With her forehead resting on his shoulder she turned her head from side to side. "I didn't know it could be so wonderful all over again."

"Each time will be more wonderful than the last, Antonia."

"For how long?" Her eyes were open now, watching him.

Ross drew her closer, holding her next to his heart, his lips brushing against her hair. Thunder whispered in his ear. Lightning shimmered in his eyes. The promise of rain.

And Antonia was waiting for his answer.

"For as long as we have to love."

Nine

Orelia opened the oven of the wood stove to check her browning biscuits. Clucking in satisfaction she wiped her hands on her apron before turning back to a pan of frying chicken.

The rain had come and gone, and with it the snow. The sun was shining, the temperature rising. It was a good day to be out-of-doors, but Antonia sat on a tall stool, watching the old lady move spryly around the kitchen, listening to stories of her life. Down by the stream, she could hear the thud of an ax as Ross felled the copse of trees threatening the dam.

She sat listening to the reassuring sounds before returning to their conversation. "It still amazes me, Orelia, that with your schooling you ended up here on this lonely mountain."

"I loved my Lon, this was his land."

"But you were a teacher!"

"I was that. Taught some of Lon's brothers and sisters sent down to board in the valley. 'Twas when he came down to see about them that he caught my eye."

"I can understand that, but why didn't the two of you settle there? Why here in this godforsaken place?"

"First, it isn't godforsaken," Orelia admonished. "Second and most important, it was his home."

"But there's so little here." Women's liberation and modern ideas aside, Antonia couldn't conceive of a woman living in such isolation for more than seventy years.

"Lon was here." The old voice reminded quietly. "Men are strong, girl, but sometimes women have to be stronger. Make no mistake about it, Lon would have moved to the valley if I'd asked him. But I saw early on what it would do to him." She patted Antonia's shoulder, leaving a streak of flour. "The land was in his blood, it was a part of him. Without it, he wouldn't have been the man I loved."

"You made the sacrifice, because you were stronger?"

"It wasn't a sacrifice, but in this I was stronger."

"Then teaching wasn't so important to you?"

"I loved teaching, but I loved Lon more. He would've come to the valley or anywhere else for me, but it would have changed him." Dishing up the chicken, she wrapped it in a cloth and packed it in a basket. "Would you ask your man to do something that meant he wouldn't be that man anymore?"

"I don't know," Antonia answered honestly.

"I think you do. Or you will when the time comes."

"I wonder." Antonia's eyes strayed to the window. Ross was only a vague image beyond the distorted glass. When she'd awaked alone in their bed it was to the sound of coffee perking. He'd brought her a steaming cup, kissed her, teased her for blushing and wished her a good day as he left the cabin. He'd spent the morning outside and Antonia knew it was to give her time to come to terms with the night. Though she was grateful for the thoughtfulness and the space, she missed him dreadfully.

"You'll see."

"I beg your pardon?" Antonia forced herself to look away from the window.

"I said, you'll see." Orelia stopped as she realized that Antonia's attention had wandered again. Smiling to herself she took the biscuits from the oven. As with the chicken they were wrapped in a checked cloth. Next in the basket were sweet potatoes that baked with the biscuits, a jar of strawberry preserves, a cake of butter. Lastly, going to the cistern at the back door, she drew out a bottle and wiped it dry. Tucking a tablecloth around all of it, she passed the basket to Antonia.

"And this," she said as she folded a quilt over Antonia's arm. "You'll need it for the wet ground. Now, you've paid your dues to your hostess, so scoot. It's a nice, warm day and your man's bound to be working up an appetite. Take him down to the meadow by the crick and spend the afternoon. I reckon by now the dam's safe and he's split a powerful lot of wood. Enough to get me through the summer's cooking and part of the winter."

"Won't you be coming with us?"

"Now why in creation would I do that?" Orelia chuckled. "I don't think your man would thank me for the intrusion, and I have plenty to keep me busy here."

Antonia knew better than to argue. Orelia would be busy, for without fail, part of her afternoons were spent polishing the furnishings Alonzo Cade had crafted for his bride. He'd built the tall four poster in the single bedroom, Orelia's rocker, tables, chairs, chests scattered throughout the house.

All of them had been his gift to her. His labor of love. Caring for it every day for seventy years was Orelia's.

"Are you sure you'll be all right here alone?"

Orelia hooted in laughter. "I have been for years. Now, go to your man before the chicken gets cold and the wine hot."

"Thank you, for everything." Antonia hugged her and eagerly whirled away. Though her step was quick, anxious, at the door she halted. "Orelia. About Ross." A pause stretched into awkwardness as Orelia waited. This confession wasn't as easy as Antonia expected. "He isn't really my man, you know."

"Because a minister hasn't read the words over you?" Orelia made a dismissive gesture. "Doesn't matter. By the time the circuit preacher arrived to read over Lon and me..." She tented her hand a foot beyond her abdomen. "I was out to here with our first babe. At which point do you think he became my man?''

"I, uh, see what you mean."

"Good, now go. It isn't kind to keep a hungry man waiting. No matter what he's hungry for.''

"Orelia! Such thoughts!" Antonia's cheeks bloomed in a crimson blush as she dashed out the door.

The sun was high. Shadows shrank to tiny puddles beneath trees scattered by the stream. Temperatures that had plummeted unseasonably, now rose just as unseasonably. The ground was only a little muddy and tiny ice floes that cluttered the stream had disappeared.

Shirtsleeve weather, Orelia called it. But Ross wore no shirt. He'd stripped to the waist, and tied a bandanna around his forehead. Somewhere along the way he'd managed to shave. As she stopped by the stream watching, she imagined him crouching there, unmindful of the primitive conditions, scraping his beard away with Alonzo Cade's straight razor. Sweat soaked the bandanna and dripped from his clean-shaven chin, running in rivulets over his body. The sheen of moisture lent his skin the look of polished marble, accentuating every line and angle. Antonia's fingers tingled with the memory of those muscles rippling under her touch.

He was grace in command as wrists flexed, arms raised, and the ax plunged deeply into wood. Splinters flew like sparks. The rending of wood echoed sharply through the tiny hollow, waning with each repetition. Then, in the silence, every fiber and tendon straining, he pulled the blade free. There was an unstudied naturalness in each move, an easy skill and power, acquired in the years he'd labored with his brothers, wringing their livelihood from McLachlan forests and land.

Antonia stood at his back content for now just to look at him. But when he flinched and, laying the ax aside, pressed his fingers to his eyes, her heart lurched in panic. "Ross!"

He whirled to face her, his red-rimmed eyes lighting with a smile. "Antonia, love, I didn't hear you come up."

Basket and quilt went flying as she brushed aside his pleasantries and rushed to him. "Your eyes!" She touched his brow, feeling the heat of him beneath her cold fingers. "Are you ill? The concussion?"

His expression was puzzled, then he began to smile again. Taking her hands in his, resting then against his damp chest, he said ruefully, "Nothing so drastic. Though your reaction makes me wish I could claim it."

"Don't say that. Not even to tease."

"Honey, it was just a little sawdust. It wasn't going to kill me, anyway, it's already gone." When he laughed, Antonia bit her lip and looked away. "Hey, what's this?" Startled, he lifted her face with their twined hands. At the sight of tears shimmering in her eyes he was instantly contrite. "Would you care so much if I were injured?"

"You know I would." Her gaze was steady, meeting his now, the gray irises almost iridescent.

He sighed and brought her hands to his lips. He had known, but he'd wanted to hear. He hadn't reckoned with his physical response to his granted wish. Watching her over their clasped hands, nipping at her knuckles with his teeth, soothing the bite with his tongue, he wondered how *she* would respond if she knew he wanted to lie with her, here, now, on the wet ground. Lord, he wanted it. Every corner of his mind ached for it, his body demanded it. But the common sense he clung to warned Antonia wasn't quite ready for such animal passion. Not yet.

Putting her away from him while he could, he directed his interest to the basket. "What have we here? Food, I hope?"

"A feast, prepared by Orelia. For my man."

Ross laughed, delighted with her, with the possessive expression. "Then, my woman, as soon as I wash the wood chips and sweat away, and get my shirt, we'll find a dry place for our banquet." Striding to the stream he knelt on the bank, scooping water in his palms, sluicing away the evidence of his labor.

Unsettled by the desire in his face, Antonia stood mesmerized as he washed. Water glittered like beads of amber on his tanned skin, and in his hair. Snug khakis pulled tautly over his thighs were the same bronzed color of his body. He could have been naked crouching there. A monochromatic illusion, savage man at his ablutions.

Like the savage, Ross belonged to the land, and the land to him. He would be strong wherever he went, and she would love him. But not as much as she loved *this* man. The man for whom the land was an integral part of his soul.

"Orelia was right," Antonia admitted in an undertone to no one, for there was no ear to hear, no heart to break but her own. "I can't ask that he leave this."

Unable to bear anymore, she busied herself with righting the tumbled basket. She was tucking the cloth around the wine when his hands circled her waist, lifting her to her feet, pulling her back against him in one insistent move. His arms locked around her, his thighs pressed against her buttocks. When he nuzzled beneath her hair to kiss her neck, his face was damp.

"You left your hair down," he whispered into the curve of her shoulder.

"Yes." Antonia leaned into his embrace, aware of every drenched and supple angle of his body.

"For me." The husky words trembled in his stillness.

"For you."

"You knew what I would want when I saw it."

Antonia nodded. "I knew."

Ross spun her slowly to face him. "Are you angel or wanton? I can't decide."

"Neither can I," she answered honestly.

"There's a place farther down the stream. It's quiet, secluded, perfect for—" Ross stopped abruptly, realizing what he was presuming, wondering what he could be thinking. Just seconds ago he'd decided Antonia was too new to passion for the brazenly uninhibited lovemaking he was about to suggest. Backtracking, he tried to make amends. "It's a small protected field, unhurt by the cold. There's a patch of blue flowers there, smaller even than a violet, but sweeter. A slab of rock juts over the stream, like an island apart. We could spread the quilt over it for our picnic."

"Ross, darling." Antonia's fingers stopped his lips. "You're rambling, avoiding the truth when there's no need. No need at all. Why pretend that either of us is hungry for food?"

"Oh, God! Sweetheart. Don't say it if you don't mean it. I'm already half out of my mind." He reached for her, his embrace crushing. "Angel or wanton, I want you. All of you. I've dreamed of you here, in this land as primitive as the day of creation, with the breezes of spring to comb your hair, sunlight to clothe you. And I to love you."

A fitting dream for one who belonged to the land. And from the dream, for her a lover, primal, savage, handsome. Lifting her mouth for the kiss that was all the answer he needed, she whispered against his lips, "For as long as we have."

On a sun-warmed slab of rock cushioned by the folded quilt, Ross lay with his head in Antonia's lap. The remnants of their picnic had been repacked. When they'd finally redressed and swooped greedily upon Orelia's feast, consuming every morsel, the chicken and biscuits were cold, and the wine warm, but he didn't notice.

Lazily, between the edges of her open shirt, he traced the underside of her breast, fascinated as the smooth, soft nipple grew small and hard. Because he couldn't resist, he brushed the shirt from her shoulders. "I like you like this, naked in the sunlight. Only mine to see and to touch. To love."

Antonia laughed and pinched his ear. "Lecher," she grumbled, but made no move to cover herself. When he drew her head down for his kiss, she melted against him, bare breasts to bare chest, mouth gently seeking. There was sorrow in her kiss, bittersweet regret when she drew away.

Winding his hand in her hair, Ross searched her face. "What's wrong?"

Antonia laughed, convincing no one. "What could be wrong? Look around us. Once I thought just being warm would be paradise, but we have so much more. The sun, the water, your little flowers. Haven't I told you I like your choice of trysts, Doc?"

Releasing her Ross sat up. Drawing her blouse back over her shoulders he began to button it. "Sweetheart, you're a hell of an actress, but you need practice on your lies." Finishing the last button with a flourish, he drew her into his

arms and leaned with her against the rise of the stone. "Now
that I won't be distracted, suppose you tell me why you're
sad. Try the truth this time."

Antonia hugged his arms to her side, her head nestled
beneath his chin. "You know me pretty well, don't you?"

"Not well enough. Not nearly enough."

"What would you like to know?"

"I'd like to start with what's troubling you."

"It was just a mood."

"A mood, huh? Won't wash, kid. For a star, you're the
least moody person I've ever seen." His embrace tightened.
"Since you won't tell me why you're sad, I'll tell you. It goes
something like this—the rain has washed away the snow.
The trails are passable. Dare and the search parties will be
on the move again. Sooner or later, someone will spot the
plane. Am I right so far?"

"You're reading my mind."

"After the discovery of the plane, but, thank God, not
our bodies, our marked trail will be next. In a matter of
hours, Dare will find Orelia's cabin."

"Then it's back to civilization for both of us," Antonia
finished for him.

"Back to our separate lives. The lives we've both worked
so hard to create."

Come with me. Be a part of my life. The words nearly
spilled off her tongue. Instead she sighed ruefully. "We
would have been wiser not to fall in love."

"Much wiser," he agreed solemnly. "But can love be
wise?"

Cradling her head in his palm, he kissed her, wishing he
could ask her to stay. A story told at their camp fire in the
clearing was too vivid to ask that sacrifice. Ross had only to
close his eyes to see her staring into the flames, telling of the
humiliation of being judged inferior, of taking a mama's
"gift" to leave their small town and the boy who thought he
loved her. The gift, a sizable sum of money, had been in-
vested, the return used sparingly and well. A callow, untrained girl left the little southern town, returning twice, for
her parents' funerals. On a third and last visit, a polished,
sophisticated woman repaid every cent of her debt. An-

tonia called it buying back her honor. Ross, more than most, understood humiliation. On every day spent on the city street with his drunken father he understood it.

"How could I keep from loving the honorable woman a brave young girl became?"

Antonia smiled up at him, gratified that love had softened a judgment that once would have been harsh. "Poor Sonny." Distanced by time, she could pity the boy ruled so completely by his mother. "I was his little rebellion. He only wanted me because I was a challenge and because he knew his mother wouldn't approve. If she'd waited a while, he would've tired of the chase and found someone more willing and more socially suitable. Perhaps I should be ashamed of taking the money, when I never intended to be more than his friend." Her chin lifted to a defiant angle. "But I'm not.

"I couldn't have gone to college without it. Jacinda and I wouldn't have been friends. Then I wouldn't have met you."

"Wouldn't life have been dull without that explosive little meeting?"

"Not for you, Ross. You've taken your fate in your hands and made of it what you wanted. Most of us spend our lives looking for our perfect niche. You knew your place."

He'd found his place when he was a skinny boy of eleven, standing in a barn with the twins in tow. Facing Dare for the first time and daring him not to want him for his brother, Ross had known where he belonged. Jacinda told her the story long ago, explaining the closeness the McLachlan brothers shared and how special Ross was to all of them.

In the midst of her wrangling with Ross, Antonia had admired the spirit of the child. Until she loved him, she hadn't understood the strength of the man he'd become. "Since the first moment I met you, you were always so sure of yourself."

"You're saying I was smug, are you?"

Antonia laughed. "Maybe a little."

"How you must have hated me."

"I tried," she admitted. "It didn't work."

Ross twined his hands with hers, his thumb stroking her palm. Was he any better than Sonny's mother? Hadn't he judged her as unfairly? But in the end the perfect revenge was Antonia's. "So," he murmured against her hair, "since you couldn't hate me, you set out to drive me out of my mind."

"And did I?"

"Completely bonkers."

"You hid it well."

"Then maybe I should come to Hollywood, take up your profession." In the wake of her startled gasp, when she could least dissemble, he demanded, gently, "Tell me why you're sad."

Antonia caught her lip between her teeth. The answer burned like a brand across her mind. *Because you can never come to Hollywood. Because you are what you should be, where you should be. Because I am Antonia Russell, no more, no less.* Sad truths.

She looked out over the meadow, at bright, tender tufts of leaves on bare limbs. She looked at the meadow with the stream winding through it, and at the blue blush of tiny flowers. Alonzo Cade belonged here. The woman who loved him understood. "I was thinking of Orelia."

"To come from such different backgrounds, you share a special rapport."

"Not so different in some ways. She's very much like my great-grandmother. Nana was that wonderful person every small child should have, as Dare had his Gran. Orelia speaks as Nana did, thinks as she did. The lace and the quilts are like hers." Antonia's hand tightened in his. "Even her special occasion candles are the same."

"Lily of the valley," Ross murmured, remembering the fragrance and the woman who had come to him wrapped in it. So haunting, so beautiful, he would carry the memory with him forever. "Orelia made the candles?"

"Yes." Drawing his hand to her lips, Antonia brushed a kiss over his fingers. "I'll miss her."

"So will I."

"Do you think she would come with us when we leave?"

"No, love."

"She could die here all alone, Ross."

"She isn't alone, Antonia. Alonzo and all her babies are there on the hill beyond the cabin."

"With an empty grave and a marker for the son who was lost in battle in the Pacific." Orelia's only child who lived to adulthood, but not long enough to bring home a wife who would wear the rose gown made especially for her.

Ross only nodded and drew her closer.

"What will become of her when she can't make her garden and gather her crops?"

"I'll look after her," he promised. "Nothing I can do would ever be enough to repay her for what she's done for us."

"At first I didn't understand how it could be, but she's happy here."

"She made her choice long ago."

"And never regretted it. It must be wonderful to love so completely and be so content in it."

Ross said nothing. He had no answer for the wistful whisper. Orelia and Antonia were women of a kind, but of different times. Orelia had made her choices. Now Antonia must make hers. He could only hold her and love her for the little time she was his. When the time came, he would let her go.

The afternoon shadows grew long. The sun touched the rim of a mountain. In silence they watched the beginning of sunset. One more precious day was ending. In rare contentment, the sort she had envied, Antonia had sat within the shelter of his arms and dreamed of what could never be.

"It's time, love." Ross put her from him and stood, bringing her with him. "Orelia will be waiting."

"With a wicked smile and supper."

"Which she might discover she's too weary to stay awake for."

Antonia laughed, her mood forgotten. She hooked the basket over her wrist while Ross folded the quilt. She was too happy with this day, with him, to dwell on the loneliness of the future.

"Ready?" Ross waited for her nod, then leaped from the granite slab and reached for her. With his hands at her waist he swung her down, kissing her one last time. "There were search planes over the next sector early this morning. By tomorrow or the next day they should be sighting the wreckage.''

Antonia felt guilty at the surge of regret she felt. There were friends and family beyond the mountain wondering and worrying about them, and all she could think of was the little time she had left with Ross. "How long will we have?''

"Three days, maybe four. Depends on how long it takes to get a helicopter in to land on the peak. After that it's just a matter of following our trail or finding Orelia's cabin from the air.''

"Can the helicopter land in the meadow?''

"Weather permitting, yes.''

Three days, maybe four, and Ross would go back to his life and she to hers. But Antonia knew it would never be the same. The woman who returned to her old life would not be the woman who left it. One could not look death in the face and live to tell of it without consequence. One could not love and be loved as she and Ross had and remain unchanged. Whatever their waiting lives held for them, she would be richer for these days.

"Three days, or four," she whispered. "Ross, let's not waste a minute of them.''

"Not a minute, love, I promise.''

Arm in arm he walked with her through the meadow and over the stepping stones to the other side of the stream. At a bend in the trail leading to the cabin, he looked back. In the meadow where blue flowers hid beneath the grass, broad, spiked leaves of dark green were already unfurling. Soon white, bell-shaped flowers would dance in the wind. Lily of the valley, sending up their fragrance of remembered love. And only Orelia would know.

"There." Ross tapped the last shingle into place. "That should do it." Sitting back on his haunches he surveyed his handiwork. The wood-shingled roof of Orelia's cabin was a patchwork of old and new squares. The new shingles he'd split and riven from a fallen cedar with a poleax, a wedge and a maul were rough and raw against the smooth wood Alonzo Cade had cut more skillfully. The cruder replacements would serve to seal the leaks through summer storms and winter snows and, in time, would weather until the new blended with the old.

The farm needed an able man's hand. In the three years since Alonzo's death there had been no one to see to it, or to Orelia. But soon there would be a multitude who would be eager and even honored to care for her. He would be forever in her debt, and one McLachlan's debt was every McLachlan's to repay.

And then there was Antonia.

From his rooftop seat, he looked to the garden plot he'd plowed with a metal contraption called a wheel horse. Which was exactly what its name said: a wood and metal plow with a wheel where a horse should have stood. Powered and guided by whatever hand gripped its splintered handle.

Antonia bent over the wobbling furrows planting and covering seeds. As he watched her digging in the soil, he remembered the perfection of hands that were rough now, with ragged, broken nails. As with her face, she dismissed their sad condition, preferring to concentrate on other matters. For Antonia, helping Orelia prepare for the seasons ahead was more than a chore. It was a matter of respect.

He watched her bend and straighten, her body like a swaying bow. Had any garden ever been more lovingly planted?

"City girl," Ross murmured, "with your roots in Georgia clay." She'd never been more beautiful. Sequins and mascara and blush became her, but not nearly so much as jeans and sunlight and laughter. He'd never heard her laugh so much as she did working side by side with Orelia. There was some country in the city girl yet.

As if she felt his gaze, she stopped in her task and looked up at him. With a smile and a wave, she awakened the desire that never slumbered more than lightly. Ross held Alonzo Cade's hammer in a punishing grip. He had no defenses against this woman who considered her honor lost until a debt from her youth was paid. Who would not barter virtue for success in a land where success at any cost was the greater prize.

Antonia Russell, the startling, unexpected woman, who had never known or loved a man until him.

"Antonia, what am I going to do with you?" he asked aloud, while he knew the question was really what would he do without her?

With an ache deep inside him he watched her in her labor. Substance and shadow beneath the afternoon sun, the hand of the first meeting, the hand of the latter in rich dark soil. The sky above him was clear and cloudless. The caw of crows seeking shelter from spring's zealous burst of heat drifted from their forest roost. In his bones, like sorrow that had no solace, Ross sensed the warning timbre of change.

Drawing a long, hurting breath and brushing the sting of sweat from his eyes, he collected the last of the tools scattered beside him. Walking the crest of the roof to its edge, he climbed down the ladder and stepped to the ground.

His tread was heavy as he crossed the plowed land to Antonia.

"Hello." Antonia smiled up a him with her lips, but her eyes were solemn.

She knelt in loose soil and in her hand she held the precious seed Orelia had harvested. Long, sweat-soaked strands of hair had escaped the single braid that trailed down her back and were plastered to her face and neck. A streak of dust had smeared over her cheek, barely skirting the pink, healing scar at her temple. A familiar purple shirt clung to her shoulders and breasts, the moist cloth lying like a second skin over the voluptuous curves, marking with its wetness the darkly, delicate thrust of their crescents.

Each day he thought she couldn't be more desirable, and each day she was. Reaching for her, taking her by her shoulders he lifted her to her feet. "Hello yourself," he murmured as he drew her closer, his hands curling around her, one at her waist the other at her neck. He teased her lips with his own, drawing quickly but reluctantly away. "You've been working a long time."

"Not nearly so long or as hard as you. Orelia was nearly in tears when she saw the plowed field."

"Where is she now?"

"In the cabin making a special cake from the apples she dried last fall. She's overwhelmed by all you've done. She swears the farm hasn't looked this good since her Lon was in his prime."

"Little enough, when balanced against her hospitality."

"I wish she weren't so isolated."

"I know," Ross agreed. "We're leaving her in good condition for now. Later one of us, my brothers or I will come up this way periodically. Shouldn't be more than a few hours' flying time to the nearest small airport."

Forgetting her soiled hands she'd held tucked behind her, Antonia wrapped her arms around him and leaned against his broad, hard chest. His skin was damp, but he smelled of sunlight and Orelia's spicy lye soap. He wore faded jeans today, and a blue bandanna, but his chest was bare against her cheek as she listened to the strong rhythm of his heart. Letting its beat sweep from her mind the nagging sound that droned little more than silently in the distance.

"She'll be lonely for a while." Her words flowed like a breathless kiss over his skin. "After we're gone."

Ross tilted her face to his. "You know, don't you?"

"That it's over?" Antonia caught her lip between her teeth. Her lashes swept down over her cheeks shielding her from him. Reaching deeper and deeper within herself, she found a reserve of strength she had hoped was there. When she looked at him again, her eyes were bright, but the tears that gathered there would go unshed. "At first I didn't understand. There was only the vibration in the earth. Then I realized what I was feeling was the percussion of a helicopter's rotor."

"Flying low through the gorges."

"They've found the plane and our trail, and now they're searching for us."

"The sound transmits like blows striking the shelf of granite that commonly runs though these mountains." Biting off his rambling lecture, he clasped her closer, facing the truth. "The chopper's probably working in tandem with a ground party that's following the trail we marked."

"We should be rejoicing. Our ordeal's almost ended."

"Almost."

"Your brothers and Jacinda can stop worrying at last."

"At last." Stroking a line beneath her scar with the edge of his thumb, his eyes roamed her face, memorizing every feature.

"We can get back to the lives we've carved for ourselves. To those who depend on us. Your patients, my—" Her voice broke as the strength she'd summoned failed her. "Ross, I don't want to leave."

"I know."

Her hands clutched at his sides, the nails biting into bared muscles. "Leaving or staying isn't a choice that's ours to make." The nails bit deeper. Her tone took on a note of bitterness. "The lives we've chosen, the commitments we've made are waiting."

Ross heard the hurt. For an insane moment he wanted to ask her to turn her back on the life she'd made, to forsake every commitment but that she'd made to him—the love she'd given with her body. The plea lay on the tip of his tongue, but he knew he couldn't voice it. Instead he said nothing, letting her resolve what she must, as she must.

Antonia looked around her, her attention lingering on the cabin. "I'll never forget this, any of it." The gray gaze found him. "I love you, Ross. I always will."

He heard the sound of goodbye in her words, and with it grief for what might have been. "Loving you, even for the little time we've had, is better than never loving you at all."

Antonia's gaze never left him. Ross wondered, if like he, she was doubting that bit of profound foolishness would ease the ache of a lonely heart.

"How long do we have, Ross? How much time before it's really over?"

Drawing her head back to his chest, he brushed her forehead with his lips. Holding her closer, tighter, he watched as a helicopter appeared over the tree line. The great, white machine with Patrick McCallum's logo painted on its side, passed over the meadow, circled, then returned. This time it hovered over the letter *R* spelled out in river stones in the grass. The nose of the craft dipped lower, rose and dipped again.

With a sense of loss, Ross watched as it began to descend. "We've no time left, sweetheart," he said into the sudden din of heavy motors. "None at all."

Ten

The cabin pulsed with life, with the zest and vitality of men crowded at a makeshift table of sawhorses and long boards. Above the clatter of crockery and a table laden with food prepared by Orelia, their voices rose in laughter. From her place at Ross's side, Antonia watched and listened as brothers and friends celebrated the return of one of their own.

In the years since Jacinda became a McLachlan, Antonia had learned of the strong family ties. But until now she hadn't witnessed the depth of that love and loyalty.

Dare had come as Ross said he would, and with him, Robbie and Jamie. For what were classes and concert dates when balanced against the life of a brother? In the meadow, with the dust stirred by the whirling blades of the helicopter not yet settled, brother had embraced brother, unashamedly, drawing the lost one back into the family circle. And Antonia had gone a step farther in understanding Ross, and what made him who he was.

She sat, more observer than participant, while Ross spoke of the flight, and as men grew quiet, of the crash. One after the other turned to her, watching, listening. Dare, Robbie,

Jamie, Patrick McCallum, Rafe Courtenay, David Canfield, and Hunter Slade the half-breed sculptor and master tracker, offering respect that brought a blush to her throat.

"Ross!" She protested at last. "You make too much of it."

"Being grateful for one's life is too much?" He turned to her, taking her hand in his, drawing her fingers to his kiss. "I think not." Ross smiled at her and the hush at the table grew deeper, more thoughtful.

Jamie was first to look away, first to speak. "Can you believe this guy?" He laughed and waved a hand toward Ross. "When he decides to crash his plane, correction, *our plane*, he ends up marooned with the prettiest and bravest lady in the world." Turning the full force of his charming smile on Orelia sitting at Ross's right, he drawled, "Then if that isn't enough, he discovers the world's greatest cook."

Orelia accepted his teasing with an old-fashioned grace. "I thank you for the compliment, but I can see you're a sly one with the ladies."

"He would be," his twin amended, "if the ladies of Madison hadn't locked their daughters away years ago."

"Not all of them." Jamie's grin was infectious and a somber mood passed.

The recounting of the story was done, and then the laughter. Over the last of Orelia's long hoarded coffee, the rescue party grew restless. Rafe was first to say what must be said. "It's late. If we want to get out of the valley safely, we need to leave before daylight fails." He glanced at his watch. "That leaves less than half an hour. I've some things to check before take-off. I'll wait for you at the meadow."

On cue, other excuses were made, respects paid, then Ross and Antonia were left to say a private goodbye to Orelia. She was frail in his arms when he drew her into his embrace. "I have a lot to thank you for." Over the silver hair he looked into Antonia's eyes. "*We* have a lot to thank you for."

"You'll both be back to visit from time to time?" Orelia asked in a quavery voice.

Ross hesitated, he could speak for himself but not Antonia.

"We'll be back." Antonia draped the black mink over Orelia's bony shoulders. "Until we do, will you take care of this for me?"

"Land sakes!" Orelia turned as Ross released her, her gnarled fingers stroking the luxurious fur. "Why would you leave such a pretty thing behind?"

"Because I want you to have it." Antonia recalled the times she'd seen Orelia stroking the fur, thinking her pleasure in it went unobserved. Settling the heavy coat closer around the old woman, she kissed a withered cheek. "I'd like to know that something of mine is here to remind you of me."

"Lordy! As if I need anything to remind me of either of you." A wistful look replaced the scolding frown. "Still, it would be warm against the cold."

"I hope so." Catching a bone pin that tumbled from the silver topknot, Antonia pushed it gently back in place. "I was freezing and you offered warmth. It would please me to know that I've given you the same."

Black eyes looked down at the fur, and when they returned to Antonia they were shining. "Then I'd be honored."

"Ross." Dare stood in the doorway. "I don't mean to rush you, but Rafe says we have to leave. The light's fading."

"I know. Five minutes?"

"Five then, but not a second more."

Ross's eyes closed, his hands curled into a loose clasp, his chest rose in a deep breath. A flickering candle lit the darkness of his memory, and a woman wrapped in the scent of lily of the valley came to him.

Dare was puzzled by the sudden mood. "Ross?"

The breath Ross held became a sigh. His eyes opened finding Antonia. Her smile was wistful. He knew in a glance that she remembered as he remembered, that she felt the need, the loss. But nothing had changed. Nothing could. There was no need in wishing what happened between them here could be more than a perfect interlude.

The handsome planes of Ross's face were stark, his eyes bleak. "Five minutes and we'll be there, Dare."

"Four, now." The elder brother gestured apologetically. "It's become that critical."

Ross stooped to kiss Orelia one last time. "Take care." Then he said to Antonia, "I'll wait outside."

A minute later, as she stepped through the door, a revving engine shattered the tranquil air of the cove. Trapped by rising mountains and accompanied by its own echo, the whine battered her ears, and silenced her voice. But she had no need for words as she went into Ross's waiting arms.

There would be other partings, but a kiss given in the shadow of the cabin, saying the words aching hearts could not speak, would be their goodbye.

Ross pulled away, retreating only inches. His fingertips brushed over her hair, her skin, the dewy softness of her mouth, storing away the look and feel of her to keep with him.

Antonia smiled at him. He was her nemesis, her friend, a fierce and gentle man, a rare man. Her lover. Turning her face to his touch, she kissed his palm, then took his hand in hers. Side by side, linked fingers their only contact, she walked with him down the trail to the meadow and his waiting brothers.

"Honey, wake up." Ross waited for her to lift her head from his shoulder. "We're almost back to Madison."

Antonia hadn't really slept. Curled in the seat, with her arm tucked through his and her cheek lying against the cushioning muscles of his shoulder, she'd simply pretended. As she'd lain, feigning sleep, she'd heard of Rafe's hypothesis that a freak turn in the weather had blown them off course. She heard of Robbie's—no, she corrected herself, not Robbie, Mac—of Mac's study of vectors, then the speculative but definitive words, *wind shear.* With her eyes squeezed shut and the clamor of the helicopter roaring in her brain it all came rushing back. The horror of the breath-stealing spiral that crushed her in her seat as surely as a mail-clad fist. The scream of a dying plane. Ross, deathly still in an eerie silence.

She had relived her terror of losing him. Now it was coming to pass. Not to death and injury, thank God, but to life. Every turn of the rotor brought the moment nearer in a journey that had been incredibly short.

The helicopter made it simple, going with ease where planes could not. Skimming through valleys and past peaks in a direct route to destinations that on foot would have been winding and tortuous, requiring days. Now, when she should have been rejoicing, she fought to hold herself together. The moment she'd dreaded had come too soon. The civilized world lay beneath them, waiting to tear them apart.

Perhaps it would not be today, or even tomorrow. Perhaps not next week, or next month, or the month after that. But she knew the day would come when she would lose him.

"It's over, Antonia. We're landing."

Ross's voice was low, insistent and she knew she couldn't hide from reality any longer.

The lighted field was quiet. Nothing moved as Antonia stood in the day-bright dust. Shielding her eyes against the glare, she saw a single figure moving beyond the light. Then another, and another, and still another. First was Jacinda, with tears streaming down her face. And a step behind her, Raven and Jordana, and Hunter's wife, Beth.

Ross had led Antonia through the dust, away from the helicopter. His hand still lay on her shoulder, steadying her as she mastered her fatigue and regained her equilibrium. When she surged forward at the sight of Jacinda, he moved away, letting her go. But before she could acknowledge them, there were others, boiling out of the darkness. With cameras and notepads they swarmed around her. Reporters, throwing questions and elbows in their zeal to see, to touch, to know.

Ross was a startled step away from the pack when he realized she had no need of his protection. The bewildered look that flitted over her face was gone before it registered to any but him. Replacing it was an air of quiet commanding dignity.

The transformation was astonishing, as she changed without effort from charming urchin to magnificent lady. Dressed in slacks and silk blouse, with her hair tumbled over her shoulders and down her back, and without makeup, she was instantly the star: elegant, regal, untouchable.

With a word she restrained the small crowd as none of the men rushing to her aid could have done. Not even Rafe with his hard, cold smile, not Patrick with his massive, imposing size.

Ross wondered where the rabble had come from, how they'd known to be here at this moment, but Antonia spared no time pondering or questioning. With the lessons learned from experience she went straight to the matter of their interest.

"Gentlemen." With a nod she included the lone female in the pack, "And Ms. Harrison, I know you all want your story, and you shall have it. But not tonight." Then firmly, allowing no time for argument, she continued. "For now you will have to content yourselves with the bare facts. I was a passenger in a private plane that crashed in the mountains more than two weeks ago. The pilot and I survived. There were no other passengers. We were given shelter from the snowstorm by a kind and elderly woman. In time the search party found our trail and here I am. Safe, unharmed. I owe a lot to a number of people, but that's a private matter and will remain so.

"Now, if you will excuse us. We're all tired, as I'm sure you can imagine. Tomorrow, your questions will be answered as fully as possible."

"Before we go, Miss Russell, one question."

"Just one, Ms. Harrison?"

"Yes, I promise. And I think I can say I speak for all of us." Ms. Harrison glanced over her shoulder at the men who flanked her. At their murmured assent she turned back to Antonia.

"All right," Antonia agreed. "One."

"You say you're safe, and we see that you are. But you've also said you were unharmed."

"That's right, Ms. Harrison."

"Forgive me, but your face."

In instinctive response, Antonia's hand went to her face, her fingers hovering over the mark that was no longer wound, but not yet healed scar. "I had forgotten."

"How could you, Miss Russell, when you earn your livelihood with your face?"

"I'm an actress. I hope one of talent. My face is simply a part of me, beyond that it shouldn't affect who I am, or what I do. I presume your question was to be how I got the scar?"

"That was my question."

Ross stepped to Antonia's side, laying a hand on her arm. "I'd like to answer it for you. If Antonia doesn't mind."

Antonia shook her head. "This isn't necessary."

In a habit as old as her wound, he traced a parallel path above it. "I think it is. The sooner it's done, the sooner you can get some rest." Turning to the waiting reporters, aware of the sudden leap of interest, he began. "My name is Ross McLachlan. I was pilot of the plane that went down. Miss Russell slashed her face on torn metal of the cockpit while saving my life."

A whisper of surprise rose from reporters and friends alike. Ross waited until the reaction calmed, then began his story. He spoke succinctly and without embellishment, but when he was done, not one reporter doubted that were it not for Antonia, Ross McLachlan would not be standing before them in the late hour of this April night.

"I'm sure you can understand that we're tired and want to spend time with our families and friends. Your question has been answered, and tomorrow, or the next day Antonia...Miss Russell, will speak with you at greater length. You've given your word that you'll ask nothing more until then. These gentlemen standing at my back and I expect it to be honored."

Any reporter worthy of the title recognized the impressive assembly indicated. If Antonia's bearing and Ross's suggestion hadn't been enough, sheer size aside, the mere presence of men the caliber of Patrick McCallum and Hunter Slade should've been enough to discourage the most persistent. If more persuasion was needed, there was the aura of danger natural to David Canfield and Rafe Courtenay. For good measure there remained the McLachlans, good men, with strength and reflexes honed by years of grueling labor.

They were dismissed. With his arm around Antonia, Ross walked with her to Jacinda. If there were hints of dissent they were silenced by one muttered comment and its reply.

"The bloody search party reads like a page from Who's Who."

"A dangerous Who's Who. I don't know about the rest of you guys, but I'm going back to the boarding house, file my story and hit the sack."

In twos and threes they drifted away. Ross and Antonia were free to be with the people who loved them.

"I had forgotten what a lovely house this is."

"It's been four years since you were here." Ross commented as Antonia roamed the room, touching the things that were his, familiarizing herself with the changes he'd made in the house that had once been Jacinda's.

"It's different now. Stronger, bolder. More masculine."

Ross chuckled. "I hope so. Though I never thought Jacinda's style was exclusively feminine."

"It's more than that." Antonia searched for the words. "It's more an absence of women." And then she knew. "There's been no woman here long enough to leave an impression."

"There's been none at all." Ross moved to the window overlooking the backyard and the stream that flowed through it. "When one gets past college age available women are hardly growing on trees. Then, my profession isn't exactly conducive to enduring relationships. At the great age of thirty-three, I've discovered I'm not the type for one-night stands."

Antonia turned in place, letting the treasures Ross surrounded himself with blend into a rich mural. "No woman has *ever* stayed here for a night?"

"Only one."

"Me."

"Does that surprise you?"

Antonia stopped turning, her gaze meeting his. "It doesn't surprise me, but it makes me happier than I have a right to be."

"Be happy, Antonia." Ross opened his arms, waiting until she came into them. Holding her, he whispered against her hair. "Don't ever be sad or ashamed of any part of what you feel. Not after what you've given me."

"My virginity?"

"No, sweetheart, your love. It pleases you that there have been no women in my home but you. Would it change how you feel about me if there had been?"

"Nothing could change how I feel."

"Then you understand when I say it pleases me that you've had no lovers before me?"

Antonia held his gaze a moment longer. In their darkened gray depths he saw she truly understood that if she'd had one lover or a dozen, he would feel as he did. After a moment she began to smile, then she laughed. "Wouldn't the tabloids have a field day with that little tidbit?"

"Should sell a record number of copies."

"I wonder. For once no one would believe them." The laughter died. "No one ever wants to believe in something good."

"I believe in something good." Ross pulled her to him. The shirt she wore was his, and beneath it nothing at all. "There's a press conference at five, dinner at Jacinda's at seven."

"Dear Jacinda. I don't think I've ever seen her quite so pleased with herself." Antonia hadn't forgotten the look of delight on her friend's face when Ross assumed as naturally as breathing, that Antonia would spend the remainder of her time in Madison with him in the house at Seventeen Magnolia Street.

"Or so worried that her matchmaking had caused tragedy. I'm only thankful that she tricked you into going with me. The wind shear would have happened, and the crash. After that, without you nothing would have been the same."

"Don't." Antonia laid a finger over his lips.

Ross kissed her finger as she moved it away. "You're right, that's behind us. This is a wonderful spring day in Madison. Until the conference and dinner there's absolutely nothing that requires our attention."

"Nothing?" Antonia kissed his bare chest, her hands sliding down his body to the snap of his jeans. "Could I persuade you otherwise, my love?"

"Sounds interesting. How would you go about it?"

"First there's this...and then this..." Like a kitten at play she teased him, laughing softly at each tautly drawn breath, each shudder. She was an ingenue just discovering her power. She was a wanton, sensual and sexy, plying her wiles.

She was every man's fantasy, but only for Ross.

"Enough, sweetheart. Enough." Sweeping her from her feet he took her to his bed.

Even in enchantment, neither forgot what hadn't been spoken. These were Antonia's last hours with him. She would be on a midnight flight to California.

"Have you heard from her?"

Ross picked up a pebble from his lawn and skimmed it over the stream. The first colors of autumn reflected in its depths shattered beneath the glancing blows. The splashes were like an echo. Once, twice, a third time, then no more. The water grew calm, its current barely rippling a mirroring surface. Autumn was in place again before he answered Jacinda's question. "Yesterday. I heard from Antonia, yesterday."

"She's back in California!"

"She called from Australia."

"Oh." Jacinda visibly wilted. "I'd hoped the movie was finished. She's been working nonstop for months now. It's almost as if she's in a frenzy. As if work helps her forget."

"Jacinda." Ross caught both her hands in his. "Don't second-guess her and don't suppose. She's doing what she loves. Being what she spent her life preparing to be."

"She loves you, Ross."

"I know she loves me."

"Then why didn't you ask her to stay? Why don't you ask her now?"

"I can't."

"Why not?" Jacinda turned her astonished face toward him. "When two people love each other, they should want to be together."

"But it isn't always as simple as that. I won't ask her to do something I can't do."

"Leave the life you've made. That in its way has been your salvation."

"That's a large part of it. If I'm honest, it's more than that. I can't ask her to come live my life when I couldn't live hers." Ross picked a crimson leaf from a shrub, watched the sun turn it to flame, then let it drift to the ground. "I've thought about it."

"About leaving here?"

Ross nodded. "It wouldn't work. I'd be a misfit in her life, a millstone around her neck. Glamour wouldn't become me."

"You're wrong!"

"No, honey," Ross said kindly. The decision that had been long and hard for him, would be as difficult for Jacinda to accept. "We both know I'm right."

Jacinda shoved her hands into the pockets of her trousers. With the toe of her boot she tumbled a stone down the hill to the stream. As it disappeared beneath the surface she grumbled, "I wish I could say I understood this. Then, maybe, I wouldn't feel so guilty. It must hurt to love like this. So much you must wish you'd never loved at all."

"Would any hurt be too much for you to love Dare?"

"I..." Her voice trailed away. She swallowed with an effort. "No." Then as a tear of helpless empathy spilled down her cheek she added, "Never."

Ross looped an arm around her shoulders and walked with her across the lawn. As he opened the door of her car his telephone began to ring.

"Maybe that's Antonia," Jacinda ventured. "Except it must be some ungodly hour in Australia."

"That's when she calls," Ross said, his voice suddenly low and raw. "In the ungodly hours."

"Why?"

"Because she can't sleep." With a wave he smiled—a smile that didn't reach his eyes—and raced to the house, through the open door, to the telephone.

* * *

Antonia put down the news clipping she was reading. The reviews were good. No, the reviews were better than good and tonight her agent planned a party to celebrate, but she wasn't interested. The very thought of having her hair done, and her face, then zipping herself into a creation never meant for comfort, revolted her.

Then there was Jeremy Baron, a handsome golden Californian. Her constant escort in the weeks since her return from Australia. A man in whom she could summon no interest, ironically, chosen by her agent to be her latest love interest. A ploy meant to pique the curiosity of the press now that the furor of the story of the crash had died away.

In a rush of frustration Antonia surged to her feet, sweeping clippings to the floor in a flurry. She wanted to act, to ply her craft the best she could, and publicity be dammed. But, as with the casting couch she'd escaped, the party tonight was part of the game. "How can I stand it?"

Moving to the window she stood before it holding her arms tightly crossed. At her feet lay yards of concrete, acres of falsely blue water, and trees trimmed in perfect, unnatural circles. If there was a sun it was hidden beneath layers of haze.

How Ross would hate it, the hot-white concrete, the still blue water, the mutilated trees.

Closing her eyes, she leaned her head against the windowpane. It was warm, offering no cooling relief for her burning flesh. But could anything so long as she was between roles, playing the politics her agent promised would one day garner an Oscar?

Restlessly she paced the room. The clock warned that it was time for her hairdresser, but she wasn't ready. Not yet. For the tenth time in an hour she lifted the telephone from its cradle, her fingers finding the numbered keys with the ease of long practice. The connection was made. The telephone at the other end of the line rang as it had each time before, endlessly without answer. Antonia was within inches of breaking the connection when she heard his voice. Even then she was tempted to hang up. What was she thinking? What she wanted to suggest was foolish.

"Antonia?" The voice was muffled, tinny, insistent. "Answer me, Antonia, I know you're there."

Hearing his voice, even garbled and distorted, was like being touched by him. It soothed, it hurt, it made her want more. "I didn't mean to disturb you."

"You didn't disturb me, sweetheart."

"I shouldn't have called."

"I'm glad you did. Now, tell me what's wrong."

"I miss you."

"I'm sorry, but I'm glad, too." He fell silent, waiting, letting Antonia take this where she would.

"Could we meet?"

"Name the time and place, love, and I'll be there."

"Someplace away from here. Away from the prying eyes."

Ross thought for a moment. "Atlanta, tomorrow?"

"I'd like that."

"Madame Zara's, at eight?"

"I'll be there." There was so much she wanted to say. That the months since she'd seen him had been years. "Ross," she began, then knowing she couldn't burden him with her loneliness, she continued softly, "I'm sorry, I really have to go."

"Another party?"

"Am I that transparent?"

"You called."

"I usually do before parties, don't I?"

"Give my regards to Mr. Baron."

"He needs your sympathy more. I'm not good with men without a script, you know. I think I bore him."

"I hope so. Tomorrow?"

"Tomorrow." Antonia severed the connection. Tomorrow, she thought, when her loneliness would end for a while.

Eleven

Spring

In the garden restaurant, Ross sat among plants and bright flowers, listening to the babbling rush of a waterfall. At a table set for two, in a vase of crystal, one perfect stem of lily of the valley perfumed the air. Creamy damask cloth, creamy napkins, creamy flowers, completed an aura of inviolable separateness. An island of calm created by Madame Zara for two lovers who would dine, but sparingly. Whose need was not for food.

Five times they'd met here in Atlanta. Once each month since that first autumn evening when Antonia had newly returned from Australia. Even then Madame Zara, with her uncanny intuition, sensed their needs. This table became their table, held ever in readiness. Tucked away in a secluded corner of the rooftop garden, with only the sky before them, lovers could talk and touch, keeping each other always in their eyes.

No one disturbed them. No one dared the wrath of Madame Zara. Even the waiter attended his duties as if he were a ghost.

No one knew why they came here. No one asked. Not even Ross, himself, could put into words this need to meet, to see, to shed the persona of other worlds. Not even he could explain the moment, that perfect moment when he knew that she knew it was time. When he would rise, and taking Antonia's hand in his, would go with her to their suite on the floor below.

On this night Antonia was late. She'd been late in the past, but never so much as this. Ross tried not to worry. The flight was delayed, that he had discovered. For a moment he was tempted to call a cab and go to the airport, to be there when she arrived. But it was only a moment, and only temptation. Antonia hated the frenzied airport hellos and goodbyes. He would wait, however long it took.

Restlessly he picked up his empty wineglass, but when the watchful waiter surged forward to fill it, Ross waved him away. He would not drink even one sip of their special wine alone.

Water flowed, the flower surrounded him with its fragrance. The moon traversed the night sky. He sat, remembering a mountain, a cabin, a passion too intent for caution. And remembering, he waited.

"Dr. McLachlan." The waiter hovered, poised for flight. "It's late, Madame Zara wonders if you would like something. Some refreshment from the bar, or an appetizer?"

"Nothing, thank you." It was on the tip of his tongue to ask for a telephone when he sensed a change. It was nothing he could describe, he simply knew. Rising from his seat, hardly aware that the waiter faded away, he swung around.

She was there, moving through the jungle of exotic plants, a rare beauty with her hair tumbling around her unadorned face, a dress of simple elegance clinging discreetly to her body. Rare, beautiful, but with a step too gay, a smile too bright, a manner far too feverish.

She was elated, but beneath it there was sadness. Ross watched her stop to speak in genuine affection with Madame Zara. Antonia was an enigma, a wonderful contradiction. Who but she would profess an abiding aversion to children in one breath and share a natural rapport with them in the next? Who but Antonia, denizen of a make-believe world, would be first to accord Jacinda the reality and dignity she deserved by declaring Jazz a childish name, out of sync with the woman and her talent?

Who but Antonia brought laughter and tears to him at once?

"Hello." A single word, a common word, but from her lips a promise of joy, the end of loneliness. She stood before him. Tall, regal, stunning. On her pale face fatigue had stroked the finely drawn skin beneath her eyes with dusky blue. She had grown thinner and her hand, when she touched his lips with her fingertips, seemed fragile. But the look that held him, that level gray gaze, had not changed.

"Hello, yourself." Cupping her hand in his, Ross kissed her palm and drew her hand to his chest. Meeting that solemn look, he wondered if the weariness he saw was a return of the stress he'd seen nearly a year ago on a starry spring night. The first night he'd kissed her. "How are you?"

Antonia saw his frown, recognized his worry. "Tired, jet-weary, no more. I'll be fine." Her fingers laced through his, holding tightly. "Better than fine. Now."

Drawing her down to her seat, their hands still clasped across the table, Ross saw that it was true. She was too strong now for the ungoverned stress that once ruled her. But strength could no more ease the sadness he saw than it could catch the wind, or hold back the tide, or heal a rending heart.

The ritual wine glittered in goblets like liquid crystal. A candle flickered. A stirring of the air set creamy flowers swaying like tiny, silent bells. And the fragrance that haunted his dreams night and day, mingled with her scent of wild roses.

"Antonia," he whispered.

Her head tilted, her lips parted, a look of gentle askance on her face. She was puzzled by his mood, the quietness, the desperateness of his touch.

With a shrug and a discounting gesture he averted her question. "Nothing. Just, Antonia."

Antonia understood. Her name, only her name, the sound of it chased away some secret ghost. How many times had she whispered his name? How many times had the sound of it echoed in a void nothing else could fill?

Taking his hand from hers he brushed her hair from her face. The angry, livid wound had become a pale, jagged line. Once he'd thought of it as a flaw on her perfect skin, but now he saw it as simply a part of her. A mark of the woman she was. An exquisite woman, a mark of courage, and one more paradox he must unravel.

He longed to hold her, to kiss the scar and feel the flutter of her heart beneath his lips. But that would come later, when they strolled down corridors beneath the garden. In those shadowy passages with her head on his shoulder, his arm around her and their footsteps beating a halting, muffled cadence, she would whisper that she missed him, that nothing was the same without him. And in her voice he knew he would hear the melancholy of parting.

She would be happy and unhappy at the same time. But never wholly, either. Not with him.

Abruptly he pulled away, taking up his glass, cradling it in both palms. He couldn't deal with his thoughts. Their little time together was too precious to sully it with this burden. Yet he couldn't escape it.

"First there was a delay on take-off. Then we were stacked in a holding pattern waiting to land." Antonia realized he didn't hear her, that he'd heard nothing she said. Reaching out she traced the line of his fingers as they curved over the glass and, with her touch, drew him back to her. "Where are you, Ross? What are you thinking?"

He blinked, focusing. She leaned back in her chair away from the softening candlelight and in the shadows he saw fatigue more pronounced. "I'm sorry, Antonia, what were you saying?"

"You were so far away. I couldn't reach you."

"Not far away," he denied. "Here. Here with you."

"Something's troubling you." So much that it was taking him away from her.

"Maybe," he admitted. "Subconsciously."

"A patient?"

"Yeah, a patient." The lie rolled off his tongue with astonishing ease. Guilt was half a beat behind it.

"Can I help?"

"You help just by being here." That at least was not a lie. Everything was better for a while when she was with him. Ross set down the glass, flexing stiff fingers that had clutched it too tightly. Suddenly he had no patience with rituals, with this quiet honing of need. His need wanted no honing. Needed none. He wanted her and there was nothing civilized or ceremonial about it. He wanted the oblivion of her arms. He wanted to soothe his troubled soul in her. He wanted to love her.

He tossed his napkin on the table, impatience brimming over. "Dammit! Why are we spending the little time we have sitting over food neither of us wants, with a waiter hovering to pour wine we won't drink?" His hair was disheveled from the brutal sweep of his fingers. "Sweetheart, is this what you want? Is this what you fly more than halfway across the continent for?"

Antonia stared at him, startled by the passionate outburst. At first she thought it was anger, then she saw the storm of desperateness in him. A storm she could calm. Rising from her seat she bent to blow out the candle. The darkness was sudden, but not complete. Light filtered through a barrier of shrub painting shadows over shadows on the floor. Creamy cloth and creamy flowers glowed beneath the stars above the glass canopy. Her voice was soft, as soft as the night. "I don't want the food, or the wine, or this." A graceful gesture embraced the sky, the garden, the perfect table. "I only want you, Ross."

"Yesterday is done, tomorrow waits." Her fingers circled his wrist drawing him up to her. Her head was lifting as his was lowering to her kiss. Against his lips she whispered, "But we have a treasure, we have tonight."

They walked together as he'd dreamed they would, through the half-filled dining room, and down long corridors. And for a while there was no yesterday and no tomorrow. And they were lovers.

Summer

"Dr. Ross?"

Ross lifted his head from his hands. He leaned back in his desk chair and looked up at the woman who stood in the doorway. She was small and chubby, dressed in a colorful smock. Her normally merry face was solemn. "What is it, Martha?"

"Linda Harris called. Just to say hello, and to remind you she exists."

"Linda who?"

"Linda Harris," Martha repeated carefully. "Carolyn Elliot's sister. You met her when she came in with Carolyn and the new baby. She's teaching journalism at the college."

Ross shrugged. "I don't remember."

"She remembers you, and I don't think she plans to let you forget her for long."

"Don't encourage her."

"Wouldn't dream of it. I know a lost cause when I see it."

"Let's hope Miss Harris does."

"Jacinda called, too. She wondered if you were free for dinner. I told her you were. There's nothing on your agenda for the evening."

"Call her back, tell her thanks, but I can't make it."

"This is the third time she's asked and the third time you've refused." The little nurse's frown deepened. She'd worked for Ross since the day he opened his office doors. Over the years she'd watched him grow and change. She'd seen his openness and his caring for his patients. She'd seen his love for his brothers. Except for his family she knew him better than anyone. So well that when they worked with the children, she anticipated his requirements before he spoke them.

She knew his temperament, his expectations, his hopes. But she had never seen him like this, moody and withdrawn, even from his family. Especially from his family.

"Jacinda promised Brandy Alexanders for dessert." She dangled a favorite to tempt him.

"Call her back." Ross spun his chair around. With his back to her he stared out the window. "Tell her another time."

"That's what you said last time."

"Martha, please."

"All right." The woman slumped against the doorjamb. "Then would you at least go home at a reasonable hour? Maybe if you got more rest—"

"Good night, Martha," Ross interrupted firmly. "I'll see you on Monday."

Martha sighed, defeated. "Good night, boss."

The clinic, usually so full of laughter and tears, was suddenly quiet. Only the swish of Martha's starched white skirt, and the click of the lock as she closed up for the day, broke the silence.

Another summer was ending and in the Carolina foothills, the days were growing shorter. Ross sat in the darkness, thinking about the weekend that stretched before him. Antonia was in California, attending to the details of her next movie. Just beyond his window there were streams to fish and trails to hike, but he couldn't summon any interest in either.

He couldn't sit in his office all night, but he didn't want to go home. Seventeen Magnolia was haunted by a beautiful ghost, and by the conscience of a man who knew and dreaded what he must do.

Like a man old before his time, he stood wearily, collecting charts to take home. If he worked, maybe his mind would stay quiet. If he immersed himself in his patients, perhaps he wouldn't think of Antonia.

Two hours later, sitting in his study, with charts spilling over the desk and on the floor, he wondered who he thought he was fooling. Every line he read was prefaced and ended by some thought of Antonia. There was a party tonight, something she dreaded and he ached for her. Every telephone call had him grabbing for the phone, hoping it was her. And every call had been a worried mother.

"Or a worried brother," he muttered. "Worried about me." Scowling at the unread file, he put it aside. "Ross, the steady one. Who never doubted who he was or what he wanted. Until he fell in love."

Shoving out of his seat he went through the house and out the door. There was a hint of fall in air that was crisp, not sultry. Leaves of the poplar were already showing yellow, and sugar maples blushed among the green.

Sitting on the back steps, with his arms folded over his knees, Ross looked out at the land lying under the moon. Another time he would have thought it was a good time, a good place to live. But now he took no solace in it. He saw only the darkness and that the stars were cold and lonely.

As lonely as Antonia was, because of him. How much simpler life would be for both of them if she could have loved someone like Jeremy Baron. And he someone like the persistent Linda Harris.

He'd never intended to hurt her, but since he insinuated himself into the fabric of her life, it had gone awry. The sheer joy of her artistry, the wonder of creating, had dimmed. Happy and unhappy in her work, where once there had been the wondrous surge of creative energy, now there was raw emotion.

Her reviews were astonishing. Her acting moved to another dimension—stark, powerful, with a depth of feeling few could reach. Raving critics attributed it to growth, to learning. Ross knew they were catching a glimpse of her torn and aching heart.

She loved him. He never doubted it. But the anguish of constant partings, the juggling of two disparate lives, had become a destructive task.

"What do I do?" He raked a hand through his hair. "Dear heaven, what do I do?"

As from a perfectly scripted scene, the telephone rang. Ross glanced down at his watch. It was midnight in California. Antonia would be calling, this time after her party. He crossed the porch, the screen door slammed as he reached for the phone.

Her voice was breathless, sad. "I tried not to call, but I couldn't stop myself."

"How was the party, Antonia?"

"Awful. I left as soon as I could." The line was quiet, only a scratch of static intruded. "Ross?"

"I'm here, love."

"I miss you."

"I know." And he did know then what he had to do. Not just yet, but one day soon. For now, he simply wanted to cheer her up. Settling into a chair he began. "So, tell me, who arrived wearing the same gowns and what designers had better run for their lives?"

Antonia laughed. He cared not one whit for gossip of gowns and designers. "I haven't the foggiest. I only know that I love you."

"I know you do, sweetheart," Ross said again. There was grief in his voice when he whispered only to himself, "I know you do."

Autumn

Antonia sat on the terrace of her new home. When she'd fled the frenzy of celebrity life, she'd chosen this Spanish adobe perched at the edge of California's high desert country. It was small, open, sunny, with not one square of white concrete, one drop of blued water, or one mutilated tree in sight.

The seemingly barren desert that stretched before her hid a wealth of treasures. Plants, animals, time-carved canyons and wind-blown mesas. In spring it would explode into blooming color, but now it was stark and breathstopping in its desolate grandeur. The mountains that rose out of the desert were bare, but in the winter they would be capped by snow.

Unlike Ross's land, yet like it. Unconsciously she nodded and spoke aloud. "Ross would like this."

"Ross does like it."

The table beside her chair tumbled over as she rose and turned in a whirl. "Ross?" Her hand went to her breast, resting over her heart. "What...?" She was pale and shaking. "Orelia? Has something happened to Orelia?"

"Orelia's well. Dare and I were up to see about her two days ago." He didn't finish as Antonia launched herself into his arms. He hadn't meant to do it, but he found himself holding her, kissing her with a fierceness that almost hurt.

When she drew away, still holding him tightly by his arms, her eyes were shining. "When did you arrive? How did you find this place? How long can you stay?"

"Whoa! One question at a time. I've been here just long enough to rent a car and drive here from the airport. The house was easy to find. In your descriptions of it there were excellent directions." He hesitated over the last, wanting to delay the hurt that must be, if just for a little while. "I'll be flying out later this evening."

"Why so soon?"

Her disappointment ripped at him. There would be worse later. "A tight schedule." He kissed her turned-down lips; he couldn't stop himself. "Let's leave it for later. Tell me about this wonderful house."

Antonia laughed and hugged him, then moved away. "I've been riding the canyon. I look awful and I stink of horse."

"You look wonderful, and you smell of roses." His gaze swept over her. Over the loose braid and the wild, flying tendrils that escaped it. Over the faded red sweatshirt, worn as thin as cotton. Over jeans as faded and dusty boots. She was magnificent against the backdrop of desert and mountain, and more woman than he'd ever known.

His heart lurched and the cold sickness of dread spread through him. How could he ever leave her?

"Come with me." She took his hand. "There's something I'd like to show you."

He went with her down the steps of the terrace and through the winding path of a rock garden shaded by sycamores and cottonwoods. Only a few steps beyond it they were at the desert's edge. It sprawled before them, over a half million acres of it. Standing in place, turning his head left and then right, for as far as he could see the land was wild and untamed.

"It's wonderful, isn't it?" When he only nodded, she laughed. "Does it shock you speechless that the die-hard city dweller should say that?"

"I think it does a little."

"No more than it shocked me," Antonia admitted.

Ross didn't know whether to laugh or cry. Instead he damned himself that he had done this to her. That he had made her so unhappy with her life that she fled from it. He knew she wanted him to be pleased by her new home, but to him it was a sign that he must do what he had come to do.

And he must do it now, while he still had the strength.

Antonia tugged him a step farther, in her delight missing his dark mood. "This trail leads to a canyon, and in the heart of it there's a small oasis and a scattering of Joshua trees. They're usually found in the higher elevations, so these are special. When you can stay longer we'll ride there, maybe camp under the stars." She laughed again. "We can pretend sand is snow."

"Antonia." His hand closed over hers with a painless but commanding force.

Her animated chattering stopped. One look at his face and she grew solemn. "What is it? What's wrong?"

There was no way but straight to the heart of it. "I won't be back."

Her eyes were wide, surprised. "I thought you'd like it."

"I do like it. I like your home, and the desert."

"But?" Her hands were clasped in front of her, the nails biting into her flesh.

"But I don't like the significance of this."

"The significance?" Then suddenly, harshly, angry in her hurt. "What significance? I bought a home that I liked. I thought..."

"What did you think, sweetheart?"

"I don't suppose it matters now, does it?"

"No. I don't suppose it does." She was reeling as the impact of what he was saying hit her. He wanted to take her back into his arms, to hold her and tell her it was all a mistake.

"You won't be back here." Stunning gray eyes glittered with silver tears. "Nor Madame Zara's."

"No."

"And in Madison? What do we do? Pretend nothing ever happened between us?"

Ross was at a loss . . . he had no answer. "I suppose we'll play it as it goes when the time comes."

"You love me, Ross. I know you do."

"I always will."

Her lashes drifted to her cheeks. Before his eyes she seemed to shrink. Ross feared for a moment that she was going to collapse in the desert dust. Instinctively he reached for her. When his hand brushed her shoulder, she shied away.

"Don't touch me. Not just yet." She was so still, so pale, it hurt him to see her. Then she took a deep breath, then another, and color returned to her cheeks. She was a marble statue coming to life. When she opened her eyes, they were different. Not cold, or hard, just different. Not Antonia. "You've flown across the country to end our affair. Can I ask you...?" Her voice faltered, she drew another calming breath. "Can I ask you why?"

"Let's go back to the terrace."

"I'll stay here. Tell me now, Ross."

There was no delaying the inevitable, it was foolish to try. "You know why, Antonia. This isn't working. Maybe subconsciously we've known it wouldn't from the very beginning."

"Tell me how it isn't working, Ross."

"Because it's tearing us apart, dammit." He lashed out at her, angry because she would have every painful word. "Because it's killing me to see how each goodbye hurts you. Because I see your pain in everything you do now. You were always a marvelous actress, but now you aren't acting." He clasped her shoulders, shaking her. "Dammit, Antonia, do you think I can live with myself knowing that loving me is doing this to you?"

"You speak of me," she said barely above a whisper. "What about you? What is it doing to you?"

His hands dropped from her, and he took a step back. "I just told you. It's killing me."

Antonia nodded as if he'd finally said something that made sense. "So, what do we do now?"

"We put our lives back in order and go back to being who we were."

Her gaze held him. "And do we forget?"

It was Ross's turn to close his eyes. His turn to draw a calming breath. "No," he said at last. "We never forget."

"If you don't mind, I'd like to be alone now." Her arms were crossed protectively over her breasts as if she'd been struck. "There's nothing more to say, is there?"

"Nothing." Even though he agreed, he waited for her to speak again, but she only turned away. She had withdrawn from him, withdrawn to deal with the terrible thing he'd done to her. Ross hoped that one day she would see it was for the best. Then, perhaps, she would forgive him.

After a moment he turned, too, following the path through the garden of stones. At the terrace steps he paused. "Antonia?"

She didn't turn or acknowledge him in any way.

He wanted to tell her again that he loved her, that he always would, that he was sorry it had to be this way. Instead he simply said, "Goodbye."

He didn't wait for an answer.

Antonia hated goodbyes.

Winter

"How is he?"

"If you want to know how I am, Dare, ask me. I can answer better than Martha."

As Martha scurried away, or more correctly, as Martha ran for cover, Dare turned a critical eye on his brother. Ross looked thinner, grayer, older. "Jacinda dispatched me to bring you to dinner. I'm not to take no for an answer. The twins and Tyler haven't seen you for weeks, and your favorite sister-in-law misses you."

"Thanks for the invitation." Ross smiled, but it wasn't the smile of old. "But you're not fooling me."

"Why should we try to fool you?"

"Dare, I know Antonia's latest movie is opening in Atlanta. I know she'll be there. I know that you and Jacinda and the children are going. I hope you have fun. Let's leave it at that."

"You won't see her?"

"I can't, Dare."

"If you love her so much that you can't even see her, then why aren't you with her? She loves you as much. You're making both of you miserable acting like a stubborn Scot."

"It's for the best."

"If this is for the best, then by damn, I don't ever want to see the worst."

"She's a sure thing to win the Oscar this year." Pride throbbed in Ross's voice. The first honest emotion Dare had seen in months.

"Good, I hope she wins it." Dare lashed out at him. "Maybe it will keep her warm through the lonely nights."

"She'll find someone else soon."

"Will she? Will you?" Dare leaned closer. He loved his brother, but right now he was so angry he wanted to hit him. "Tell me, Ross, who gave you the right to play God?"

"I never—"

"Didn't you?" Dare ignored Ross's shocked face. "The lady had a choice, you know. You always said she did. Then you took it away from her."

"I didn't," Ross whispered.

"You did. As cruelly as any man could."

"Dare, I didn't intend—"

Dare stopped him with a hand clasped over his shoulder. "I'm not the one you should explain it to. Give it some thought. Deal with it. In the meantime, I'll explain to Jacinda that you won't be going to Atlanta, or coming to dinner."

Dare left him standing alone in his office, with winter's gloom gathering around him.

Creamy damask gleamed in candlelight. A creamy bouquet of flowers filled the crystal vase. With a carefully groomed hand Antonia lifted her wineglass and drank. Then setting it aside, she stared at the night sky. Beyond the sip of wine she didn't move again. She didn't acknowledge the waiter's solicitous questions for she didn't hear them. Nor did she hear the soft buzz of curiosity that surrounded her. She was lost in a world she was finally admitting could be no more than a memory.

Slowly, painfully, she drew her eyes from the sky. She had hoped and waited for the impossible. Sadly, she sighed, and in a graceful move she rose, tossing a black fur over her shoulder. No one stopped her, no one approached her and no one stared as she made her way to the door.

At a tall marble counter she paused, thanking an old friend.

"He will come," Madame Zara insisted.

"No." Gray eyes glittered but there were no tears.

Old fingers found the scar at Antonia's temple. "As surely as you bear the mark of valor, he will come."

There was more but Antonia lost the thread of conversation. It was too painful. She heard somewhere, someday, and then summer. But none of it reached her, not even her own conditioned responses. Madame Zara meant well, but it was more than she could stand.

"He won't come," she said, ending it. "This was my private goodbye. Tomorrow I go on with my life." With a wave of farewell, she moved away. At the door she paused for one last look. For one last memory. She drew a deep breath, and her memory was of a spring flower. Lily of the valley. Ross's favorite.

Ross.

The room blurred. She saw the dance of a dying fire, heard the sound of his laughter, and his arms guarded her against the cold. But there was no fire, no laughter, and his arms would never hold her again.

Suddenly aware of the secret looks, the whispers, she lifted her head a regal inch. Her goodbyes were done, there was no reason to tarry.

With a shattering heart and a flourish of mink, she stepped through the door into the rest of her empty life.

Twelve

—

Spring ... once more

"**W**ell now, young lady, what are you doing fooling with Solita when you should be in Beverly Hills getting ready for your big night?"

"There's plenty of time for that, Tex." Antonia continued to brush her lathered mare. Undisturbed by the grumpy observation, she grinned at the old cowman over the horse's back. These private stables were his, established decades ago. Thanks to his foresight he was a wealthy and influential man. Despite his wealth, or perhaps because of it, he still liked to dress the part of a cowboy and muck about in the stables. In the months Antonia had lived in the desert, she and the irascible eccentric had become fast friends.

"Calling it a little close, aren't you?" Tex Blackwell was not to be mollified by her offhand answer. "The big shindig's three nights away. You should be back in that little pied-à-terre you keep in town, fussing over yourself. Instead you're riding in the desert for hours on end, or piddling here in the stables, then scrawling pretty words on paper till the wee hours of the morning.''

Antonia laughed and looked down at her sweatshirt and jeans. "In other words I need to fix up a bit."

"Wouldn't hurt. Lord knows I think you're prettiest just like you are, a class act even in grungy jeans. But Saturday's a whole different matter. You oughta be pulling out all the stops. Out sophisticating the sophisticated. Hell, anybody'd think this award means nothing to you."

"It isn't mine yet."

"It will be. When you go home to that fancy little dollhouse in the Hills after the brouhaha, you'll be taking an Oscar with you." Tex pushed back his hat and fixed her with his cool blue stare. "Too bad you won't be taking a real-live hot-blooded man with you, too. Somebody like that goodlooking feller from back East."

"Don't, Tex. Don't make me sorry I talked to you about him." Antonia concentrated on her task, hoping Tex would have one of his rare tactful moments and let the matter drop.

"Talk!" he exclaimed. "Jawed my ear off is what you did. And soaked my shirt, *after* nearly killing this horse trying to exorcise something that won't be exorcised."

"That was a long time ago."

"Yeah, and the only thing that's changed is that you hide the hurt a little better. Deep down inside, no matter how much that writing therapy has done for you, you're as miserable without him now as you were months ago."

Antonia stopped her brushing and leaned her forehead against Solita's neck. "Is it that obvious?"

"Only to anybody with eyes. 'Peers to me it ain't going to get no better till you face some facts somewhere besides on paper," Tex observed, slipping into the exaggerated homespun attitude he affected when he wanted to make a point. "You need more in your life than movie roles, a horse and an old ex-Texan."

Solita snorted and nudged Antonia impatiently. Obediently she resumed her brushing. "I suppose that's your way of telling me I need to quit hiding in the desert and do something about my life?"

"That's what I said, ain't it?"

"More or less."

"Take a minute to look at the truth of the whats, the whys and the wherefores that brought you here. Hell, while you're at it, ask yourself why you even named your damned horse a lonesome sort of name. Solita." He snorted much as the damned horse had. "Latin for solitary."

"Careful, Tex, your education's showing. Mustn't have that, you old faker. It might spoil your image." Even in her lowest times, this friend she'd found in the desert, a surrogate father when she needed one most, could always make her smile.

For once he didn't grin back at her. "All fakers aren't old, gal. But young or old, the worst are those who try to fool themselves. Think about it. Search your soul, face what you find honestly." Pulling his Stetson low over his forehead he nodded curtly. "I'll see you on award night. Before you and Oscar go home alone." As the last barb sank in, he nodded again and stalked away.

An hour later Antonia was in her bedroom packing a bag. When she had taken a pair of jeans from it for the third time, she admitted her mind was not on clothing. "Jeans," she muttered. "Not exactly what the glamorous Antonia should be wearing."

Swinging around she stared into a full-length mirror. The woman who looked back at her was elegant even in jeans and scruffy boots, yet anything but glamorous. Where had that other woman gone, the glamorous woman, the cosmopolitan who would have hated the desert? Had she died and been reborn on a snowy mountainside? Had she ever really existed, or was she just another role to play?

Antonia was first to admit that she had been drawn solely by ambition to Hollywood, the actor's Mecca. For a while she was beguiled by it. Mesmerized by it. Then had come the crash, and loving Ross, the turning point in her life. "But this is about more than the crash. More than facing one's own mortality," she addressed the woman who watched her coolly from the mirror.

"It's more," she whispered, "than loving Ross." She had been changing for a long while before the crash, growing disenchanted with her life. It was there all along, the emptiness, the lost illusions. Despair, manifesting itself as stress and fatigue.

"But I wouldn't admit it. Ambition and stubborn pride wouldn't let me." She heard the shock and wondered why. Flinging aside the folded jeans, she went to stand at an open terrace door. Afternoon sun slanted over the desert floor, painting hollows and canyons with purple shadows. Once she thought she'd learned to see its wild majesty through Ross's eyes. Now she knew she was seeing through her own.

She had changed. Quite without realizing or understanding, she had changed. Her values, her goals, her needs. A one-dimensional life wasn't enough. Had never really been enough.

Tex was right as always. She did need more in her life than movies, a horse and a wise old Texan. What she hadn't understood was that the choice was hers. She could play the role and be the actress, only the actress, or be the woman and have it all.

"I want it all. Nothing is impossible, I *will* have it all." With those words Antonia redeclared war. "This time, my beloved adversary, you won't have a chance. For I have the greatest weapon of all . . . love."

As she crossed the room, there was a sureness in her step, one that had been missing for a long time. Scooping her jeans from the floor and packet of papers from a small desk, she packed them into her luggage with the greatest care.

"Have you seen these?" Dare flung a random selection of newspapers over Ross's desk.

"I've seen them. Antonia looks wonderful as always." Ross didn't look up from the chart he was reading.

"Careful, brother, anyone would think you can't stand to look at her."

Ross laid down the chart, raising his eyes to Dare's. "I can't." He didn't need to admit as well that he couldn't eat, couldn't sleep, and that the joy had gone out of all the things he'd cherished most. "My punishment for playing God with her life."

Dare chose not to address the remark. "What I've read predicts she's a sure winner."

''She deserves it.''

''Should be quite a night for her, still Jacinda's troubled. When Antonia called last night, she didn't sound as happy as she should be. Jacinda and I have the solution. These.'' Dare leaned across the desk to tuck an envelope into the breast pocket of Ross's lab coat. ''A word of wisdom from Gran. 'The greatest triumphs are empty without love.'

''A wise woman, our Gran. Think on it, then use these, and be happy. Make Antonia happy.'' With an affectionate pat on his brother's shoulder, Dare grinned. ''Gotta go. The twins have 'kitchen pots' and Jacinda needs help.''

''Wait.'' Ross half rose from his chair, but Dare only waved and kept going. ''Kitchen pots,'' Ross muttered, sitting down again. ''What the hell are kitchen pots?'' Then at the top of his voice he yelled, ''Martha!''

''Here, boss.'' The little woman appeared around the corner. ''No need to yell.''

''Dare was just here.''

''Uh-huh.''

''You saw him?''

''Yep.''

''Then maybe you can tell me, what are kitchen pots?''

''That's an easy one. It's Tyler's name for chicken pox.''

''The twins have chicken pox?''

''You called in something for the itch.''

''I did?''

He saw something unsettling in Martha's eyes as she reminded, ''Yesterday.''

Ross raked a hand through his hair. ''I guess I forgot.''

Martha pursed her lips. ''I guess you did. If there's nothing else, I'll close up.''

''Thanks, Martha.'' Then he was alone again, as he was every night, dreading the solitude waiting for him at home. And the face that haunted him night and day looked out from the pages of a half dozen newspapers.

She's not as happy as she should be.

In spite of himself he picked up a paper. Antonia smiled back at him, a smile that left her eyes untouched. Ridiculous! he chided himself. This was the pinnacle of her dreams and ambitions. The recognition of talent that made every sacrifice worthwhile. She should be elated. She would be elated. This melancholy was a trick of the light.

Tossing the paper aside, he shuffled through other papers, other magazines with other poses. Her smile was always warm, always lovely. Her eyes never changed.

She's not as happy as she should be.

The sadness was there, but it had nothing to do with him. He hadn't been a part of her life for half a year. She had moved on, to other things, other people. By now he was only a faded memory.

The greatest triumphs are empty without love.

No! He rejected Gran's wisdom as he examined the pictures with painstaking thoroughness, searching for a mistake, something he hadn't seen before. There was no mistake. The gray gaze that looked back at him was ever without joy.

Jacinda and I have the solution.

Ross fumbled at the pocket of his lab coat, remembering the envelope Dare had tucked there. Drawing it out he saw it was a folder instead. In it were tickets for a morning flight to California. "Ah, damn." One hand raked his hair again as the other crumpled the tickets. Too late. It was far too late.

Bitterly he tossed the tickets into the trash. What was done, couldn't be undone. There was no need to try.

Covering his face with his hands he massaged the tender flesh of his brow. The ever-present ache circled his head like a steel band. Too many frowns, too many long hours, too little sleep. Nothing was as it had been. His perfect life had slipped through his fingers. He hadn't realized how badly awry he'd gone until today, when he'd forgotten the twins' illness, and seen pity in Martha's face.

Pity? Had it gone that far?

"We've come to a pretty pass, haven't we, sweetheart?" He stroked the glossy cheek of a sad-eyed woman. "Where do we go from here? What do we do as dreams turn to dust?"

Jacinda and I have the solution.

"It's too late." Ross lashed out, desperate to quiet the voices in his mind. "Too late."

But was it? Taking the tickets from the trash he smoothed the wrinkles from them. Why shouldn't he go to California? Why shouldn't he see her and share, at least from a distance, this special time with her?

"No reason," Ross murmured. "No reason at all." He felt a rare stir of excitement. "You'll win, Antonia, and I'll be there to see you smile."

The gauntlet of the press had been run. Those who would see and be seen had settled into their particular seats or drifted away. The glittering ceremony for which onlookers and participants had come proceeded surely, if slowly. This was the moment. The audience waited. Only the cameras moved, panning from nominee to nominee, hoping to catch that perfect moment of joy, of disappointment. A statuesque woman in silver spangles opened an envelope with dramatic flair, and the theater grew quiet. "This year's winner for best actress in a dramatic role is—" she leaned closer to the microphone "—Antonia Russell, for *In a Stranger's Hands.*"

The audience erupted around her, while Antonia sat dumbfounded. "I never truly believed," she whispered. Then laughing and crying she embraced her escort and kissed his weathered cheek.

"I believed, honey. If there was any justice in this world, you had to win." Truly old enough to be her father, but still handsome in formal dress, with his mane of silver hair shining and piercing blue eyes dancing, Tex took her hand to help her stand. When she had accepted the congratulations of those around her, he hugged her and urged her along. "Go on, gal. The rest of your life is waiting."

"The rest of my life?"

"Exactly." Tex dodged her question. "Now git."

To the sound of applause she mounted the stairs. In a dress that seemed a mist of light, with her hair loose and gleaming, she stepped to the podium. For an uncommonly long time she was silent as she looked out over the audience. When she began her voice was low, and composed. "I'm not sure that I deserve this." Antonia waited for the burst of applause to die away, nodding her gratitude for the affirmation. "I wondered what I would say. What I *could* say to you beyond thank you. Then as I came to the stage, an old friend reminded me that the rest of my life is waiting. It has been waiting for two years. But no longer. I've come tonight to thank you, all of you, for this." She curved both hands around the statue. "And I've come to say goodbye."

As she looked out over stunned and mesmerized spectators, no one spoke, no one moved, not even a whisper or a gesture. In the stillness and the silence, a single person stood. A dark-haired man, tall, handsome, immaculate in perfect formal dress. The one man who understood even better than Tex the choice she had made.

"Ross!"

Antonia was as stunned as the audience. *Ross.* He was real. He was here. The rest of her life had already begun.

What more she meant to say was forgotten. First she began to walk, then, and as he moved toward her, to run. She was in his arms, his lips were on hers, and for the first time in months she felt whole. When he drew away, oblivious of curious stares, she caressed his face. "You're real, I'm not dreaming. Who...?"

"Who shook some sense into me? Dare, with plane tickets. Then Tex, with a ticket to this shindig as he called it."

"Tex? You know Tex?"

"Not until two days ago. He's a persuasive man when he believes in something."

"He promised me my life would be waiting. He knew my life is you."

Ross lifted a hand to touch her, then folded it into a fist instead. A touch would never be enough. Not nearly enough. "Let's get out of here, so I can make love to you properly."

"Yes! Oh, yes. Then I have a lot to tell you."

"But not for a long time, sweetheart. Not for a long, long time." Catching her hand in his, to the sound of a standing ovation he led her from the theater.

Antonia rose from her bed, slipped into a silk robe and padded to the window of what she'd begun to think of as her pied-à-terre. She chuckled. Tex's words again.

Beneath the moon, concrete gleamed a ghostly white, blue water glittered in the bluer pool, and mutilated trees lined the driveway like harem guards. What had once been her world was now an alien place.

Ross's arms slid around her, drawing her back against him. His lips brushed over her hair and he held her tighter.

Leaning back against him, she kissed his bare arm. "I'll have to get accustomed all over again to how quiet your woodsman's step can be."

"I don't have to be a woodsman, Antonia. If you think Beverly Hills could use another pediatrician."

"What?"

"I said I don't have to be a woodsman."

"I heard you." Antonia was turning in his embrace, her fingers digging into the muscles of his shoulders. "Why would you even consider it?"

"Because you're here, your life is here. Because I want to be a part of it."

"I said goodbye to all of this."

Ross hooked a finger through a strand of her hair and trailed through it to the end that lay over her breast. A habit from another time. "It doesn't have to be that way."

Antonia moved out of his embrace. She couldn't think as clearly as she must when he was so near. Wandering the room, touching small mementos of her past, she pondered his words. Once this would have been what she wanted. Now she knew it was the last thing she wanted. Yet that he loved her enough to make the sacrifice had her heart singing.

But she didn't want a Beverly Hills pediatrician. She wanted the man he'd been in Madison, and in Orelia's valley.

"Beverly Hills, huh? I suppose we could live here." She waved a hand to encompass the small house, and its grounds.

"If you like."

Antonia sighed. "You would hate it, Ross."

"It's not so bad."

He looked so like a small boy with the bad taste of a lie stuck in his throat, she had to laugh. "It's ugly. And you *would* hate it. *I* hate it."

"Then what do you want, Antonia? You can't just walk away from everything you've worked to achieve. Especially now."

"I can. I have." She was moving back to him, wanting to be held again, to make love again. "You asked what I want. I want to go home."

"Home?" Ross saw something in her face that he hadn't seen in a long while. Confidence, contentment, peace. "Where is home, Antonia?"

"Anywhere that I can be with you. Where I can lie down with you at night, and wake with you in the morning. Where you are the man I fell in love with."

"Madison."

"Yes, Madison. Where our children can grow up with Dare and Jacinda's. And be a family as you and your brothers are a family."

If he weren't already in shock, this would have sent him over the edge. "Children?"

"Yeah." Antonia laughed at him, at herself. "Those squiggly, wiggly, wonderful little people who catch strange diseases like 'kitchen pots.'"

"You mean this?" Ross searched her face. He caught a breath, his eyes widening in wonder. "You really do!"

"With all my heart."

"Sweetheart." He was shaking his head. "It can't be this simple. You can't just walk away from all of this."

"I can. I have to." Taking his hand in hers, she laced her fingers through his. "Even before I loved you this life was wrong for me."

Suddenly Ross remembered a March night when he'd seen a softer, less flamboyant Antonia. When he'd discovered a real and vulnerable woman who could comfort a crying child. He remembered a look across a crowded room, and the beginning of awareness, of kindness. He remembered stress and fatigue that left her pale and trembling.

"Perhaps you're right." At last he could accept the truth. "Perhaps this particular career isn't for you, but you have too much creative energy not to channel it into something."

"There are other things I can do. Things I will do. But not yet. We have six months to catch up on." When she smiled, she smiled with her eyes. "I'd like nothing better than to dispense with all these questions and begin the catching up now, my love."

"One more question."

"All right." Antonia sighed. "But only one."

"One is all I need." Ross tilted her chin with a knuckle. His gaze swept her face, the face of the woman who had given him his life. Who was his life. "Will you marry me, Antonia, and be my love forever?"

Her answer was in her kiss, and in her touch when she drew him with her to her bed. Someday soon she would show him the manuscript. The pretty words, as Tex called them, begun as therapy, then becoming a serious outlet of her creative energy. One far more satisfying than acting.

But that was for someday. As was a visit to Tex, and Madame Zara, and Orelia, to say thanks. For now, she simply wanted to love Ross.

"For now," she whispered against his lips. "Forever."

* * * * *

Look for Mac McLachlan's story, Another Time, Another Place, December's Man of the Month, only in Silhouette Desire.

OFFICIAL RULES • MILLION DOLLAR BIG WIN SWEEPSTAKES
NO PURCHASE OR OBLIGATION NECESSARY TO ENTER

To enter, follow the directions published. **ALTERNATE MEANS OF ENTRY:** Hand-print your name and address on a 3"×5" card and mail to either: Silhouette Big Win, 3010 Walden Ave., P.O. Box 1867, Buffalo, NY 14269-1867, or Silhouette Big Win, P.O. Box 609, Fort Erie, Ontario L2A 5X3, and we will assign your Sweepstakes numbers (Limit: one entry per envelope). For eligibility, entries must be received no later than March 31, 1994 and be sent via 1st-class mail. No liability is assumed for printing errors or lost, late or misdirected entries.

To determine winners, the sweepstakes numbers on submitted entries will be compared against a list of randomly preselected prizewinning numbers. In the event all prizes are not claimed via the return of prizewinning numbers, random drawings will be held from among all other entries received to award unclaimed prizes.

Prizewinners will be determined no later than May 30, 1994. Selection of winning numbers and random drawings are under the supervision of D.L. Blair, Inc., an independent judging organization whose decisions are final. One prize to a family or organization. No substitution will be made for any prize, except as offered. Taxes and duties on all prizes are the sole responsibility of winners. Winners will be notified by mail. Chances of winning are determined by the number of entries distributed and received.

Sweepstakes open to persons 18 years of age or older, except employees and immediate family members of Torstar Corporation, D.L. Blair, Inc., their affiliates, subsidiaries and all other agencies, entities and persons connected with the use, marketing or conduct of this Sweepstakes. All applicable laws and regulations apply. Sweepstakes offer void wherever prohibited by law. Any litigation within the province of Quebec respecting the conduct and awarding of a prize in this Sweepstakes must be submitted to the Régies des Loteries et Courses du Quebec. In order to win a prize, residents of Canada will be required to correctly answer a time-limited arithmetical skill-testing question. Values of all prizes are in U.S. currency.

Winners of major prizes will be obligated to sign and return an affidavit of eligibility and release of liability within 30 days of notification. In the event of non-compliance within this time period, prize may be awarded to an alternate winner. Any prize or prize notification returned as undeliverable will result in the awarding of the prize to an alternate winner. By acceptance of their prize, winners consent to use of their names, photographs or other likenesses for purposes of advertising, trade and promotion on behalf of Torstar Corporation without further compensation, unless prohibited by law.

This Sweepstakes is presented by Torstar Corporation, its subsidiaries and affiliates in conjunction with book, merchandise and/or product offerings. Prizes are as follows: Grand Prize—$1,000,000 (payable at $33,333.33 a year for 30 years). First through Sixth Prizes may be presented in different creative executions, each with the following approximate values: First Prize—$35,000; Second Prize—$10,000; 2 Third Prizes—$5,000 each; 5 Fourth Prizes—$1,000 each; 10 Fifth Prizes—$250 each; 1,000 Sixth Prizes—$100 each. Prizewinners will have the opportunity of selecting any prize offered for that level. A travel-prize option if offered and selected by winner, must be completed within 12 months of selection and is subject to hotel and flight accommodations availability. Torstar Corporation may present this sweepstakes utilizing names other than Million Dollar Sweepstakes. For a current list of all prize options offered within prize levels and all names the Sweepstakes may utilize, send a self-addressed stamped envelope (WA residents need not affix return postage) to: Million Dollar Sweepstakes Prize Options/Names, P.O. Box 7410, Blair, NE 68009.

For a list of prizewinners (available after July 31, 1994) send a separate, stamped self-addressed envelope to: Million Dollar Sweepstakes Winners, P.O. Box 4728, Blair NE 68009.

SWPS693

MEN MADE IN AMERICA

Fifty red-blooded, white-hot, true-blue hunks from every State in the Union!

Beginning in May, look for MEN MADE IN AMERICA! Written by some of our most popular authors, these stories feature fifty of the strongest, sexiest men, each from a different state in the union!

Two titles available every other month at your favorite retail outlet.

In July, look for:

CALL IT DESTINY by Jayne Ann Krentz (Arizona)
ANOTHER KIND OF LOVE by Mary Lynn Baxter (Arkansas)

In September, look for:

DECEPTIONS by Annette Broadrick (California)
STORMWALKER by Dallas Schulze (Colorado)

You won't be able to resist MEN MADE IN AMERICA!

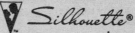

SILHOUETTE® Desire®

THEY'RE HOT...
THEY'RE COOL...
THEY'RE ALL-AMERICAN GUYS...
THEY'RE RED, WHITE AND BLUE HEROES

Zeke #793 by Annette Broadrick *(Man of the Month)*
Ben #794 by Karen Leabo
Derek #795 by Leslie Davis Guccione
Cameron #796 by Beverly Barton
Jake #797 by Helen R. Myers
Will #798 by Kelly Jamison

Look for these six red-blooded, white-knight, blue-collar men
Coming your way next month
Only from Silhouette Desire

**Relive the romance...
Harlequin and Silhouette
are proud to present**

A program of collections of three complete novels by the most requested authors with the most requested themes. Be sure to look for one volume each month with three complete novels by top name authors.

In June: **NINE MONTHS** Penny Jordan
Stella Cameron
Janice Kaiser

Three women pregnant and alone. But a lot can happen in nine months!

In July: **DADDY'S HOME** Kristin James
Naomi Horton
Mary Lynn Baxter

Daddy's Home... and his presence is long overdue!

In August: **FORGOTTEN PAST** Barbara Kaye
Pamela Browning
Nancy Martin

Do you dare to create a future if you've forgotten the past?

Available at your favorite retail outlet.

◆ HARLEQUIN® ▼ Silhouette